In keeping with the season,
Harlequin Superromance is delighted to bring
you three very special stories celebrating
Christmas past, present and future.

"Just Like the Ones We Used To Know"
by Brenda Novak
Who can deny a child her only Christmas wish?
Not Angela Forrester. A caring foster mom,
she'd even risk losing Kayla to give her the
father she's never known.

"The Night Before Christmas"
by Melinda Curtis
A modern-day Scrooge falls in love over the
course of one unexpected Christmas Eve and
learns what he's been missing out on as a
workaholic all these wasted years.

"All the Christmases To Come"
by Anna Adams
It takes a festive train ride and shared memories
of holidays past to convince a pregnant woman
to chance everything for happiness.

"And it was always said of him, that he knew
how to keep Christmas well…. May that be
truly said of us, and all of us! And so, as Tiny
Tim observed, 'God Bless Us, Every One!'"
—Charles Dickens
A Christmas Carol

ABOUT THE AUTHORS

Christmas is still a magical time for Brenda Novak, who grew up the youngest of five and has five children of her own. On Christmas Eve she loves to make, decorate and deliver homemade frosted sugar cookies with her family. Charles Dickens's *A Christmas Carol* has long been her favorite holiday story, so for the past twenty years she's collected Dickens village pieces, which remind her a great deal of the architecture of Virginia City, where this story is set.

During the holidays, Melinda Curtis fills her house with decorations and ornaments made by her three children. Someday—between her children's college years and becoming a grandparent—she plans to decorate like an adult. Until then, it's cotton-ball snowmen beside popsicle-stick mangers and clothespin Santas with globs of bright glitter.

Anna Adams loves to see snow flying in the movies, snowy holiday mugs and snow painted on her windows…because she lives in a hot climate and longs for an old-fashioned—you got it—snow-covered holiday.

ONCE UPON A CHRISTMAS
Brenda Novak
Melinda Curtis
Anna Adams

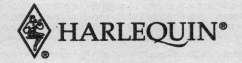

HARLEQUIN®

TORONTO • NEW YORK • LONDON
AMSTERDAM • PARIS • SYDNEY • HAMBURG
STOCKHOLM • ATHENS • TOKYO • MILAN • MADRID
PRAGUE • WARSAW • BUDAPEST • AUCKLAND

ISBN-13: 978-0-373-78125-6
ISBN-10:   0-373-78125-3

ONCE UPON A CHRISTMAS

Copyright © 2006 by Harlequin Books S.A.

The publisher acknowledges the copyright holders of the individual works as follows:

JUST LIKE THE ONES WE USED TO KNOW
Copyright © 2006 by Brenda Novak.

THE NIGHT BEFORE CHRISTMAS
Copyright © 2006 by Melinda Wooten.

ALL THE CHRISTMASES TO COME
Copyright © 2006 by Anna Adams.

CONTENTS

Dear Reader,

Virginia City is a place out of time. When I first visited there, I was completely taken with the look and feel of it, the sense that it has remained unchanged for so long. It immediately caught my imagination and begged to appear in one of my books. I'm glad it was this story, a story about Christmas.

Hopefully, as you read "Just Like the Ones We Used To Know," the town will come alive for you as it did for me.

Have a wonderful holiday season!

Brenda Novak
www.brendanovak.com

JUST LIKE THE ONES
WE USED TO KNOW
Brenda Novak

To my husband and five children,
because they make every Christmas special.

CHAPTER ONE

"MRS. FORRESTER?"

Seeing Kayla's teacher smile expectantly as she held the door, Angela swallowed hard, then straightened her spine and walked into the sixth-grade classroom. On the Friday afternoon before Christmas break, it was empty of students, yet it still smelled of pencil shavings and chalk, which evoked pleasant associations. Growing up, Angela had been a good student. But the girl she'd taken in a year earlier was struggling in school, in life.

Angela had become Kayla's caregiver so late, could she really make any difference?

That was the big question and had been from the beginning. Angela was afraid she couldn't. And she was afraid Kayla's teacher had called her in, once again, to let her know just how badly she was failing.

Trying to ignore the helplessness that

engulfed her so often lately, Angela perched uncomfortably on the chair next to Mrs. Bennett's battle-scarred desk—she knew her place in this room well—and smoothed the skirt of the designer suit she'd worn to work that morning.

"I'm sorry to bother you again," the teacher began, peering at Angela over her bifocals.

Angela pulled her heavy trench coat more tightly around her and forced a smile. "It's fine. You know I want what's best for Kayla."

"I want the same thing."

"Of course." They just approached it differently. Mrs. Bennett could be stern and rather severe. She often indicated that she felt Angela was letting pity about what had happened in the past interfere with good old-fashioned discipline. But Angela had been a foster child herself—had spent several years living in the same house as Kayla's mother, in fact—so she understood Kayla's situation well. Besides, this was Angela's first attempt at parenting. She was twenty-nine, but she wasn't married. Maybe she wasn't the best person in the world to finish raising Stephanie's daughter, but before Stephanie's mother had died, she'd given Angela guardianship because she was a better choice than any of Kayla's other options.

"What seems to be the problem, Mrs. Bennett?" She decided to ask the question and get it over with. "Isn't Kayla turning in her assignments?"

Angela knew Kayla finished her homework because they did it together. But only last Wednesday Mrs. Bennett had informed Angela that it'd been two weeks since Kayla had handed in a single paper. Angela had been shocked and worried, of course, but what made the situation more mystifying was the fact that Kayla couldn't tell her *why* she wasn't turning in the work.

"She's improving there," Mrs. Bennett said. "I'd like to see her test scores come up, but that's another issue. I called you in today because I wanted you to see something she's written."

Written? The crisp Denver winter settled a little deeper into Angela's bones. Kayla was generally excluded from the tight cliques of other girls. She kept to herself and rarely associated with the kids in her class, which had been the subject of yet another parent/teacher conference. So...had Kayla finally decided to get even with the ever-popular but cruel Barbie Hanover, who'd stolen her notebook and shown Jordan Wheeler the poem she'd composed about him?

Angela half expected Mrs. Bennett to smooth out a note detailing Barbie's lack of good qualities or some other manifestation of the intense humiliation she'd caused Kayla. But Mrs. Bennett presented her with what looked like a regular English paper. And, even more surprisingly, written across the top in red ink was a big fat A.

It was probably Kayla's first A, which should've been reason to celebrate. Except Mrs. Bennett's sober expression indicated that Angela should still be concerned.

"What—"

"Read it," Mrs. Bennett said.

Angela glanced at the heading.

All I Want For Christmas
By Kayla ???????

"She wouldn't put her last name?" Angela asked in confusion.

Mrs. Bennett gestured that Angela should keep reading.

She returned her attention to the small, cramped writing.

I suppose you want to hear that Christmas is my favorite time of year. That's what everyone else says, right? There's candy and presents and parties. There's baby Jesus and Santa Claus. Even for girls like me.

So why am I finding this stupid paper so hard to write? I should just copy someone else, someone normal. I can hear the people all around me. I want this...I want that...I'm getting a new cell phone, a new TV, a new dress. Barbie sits next to me and wants an iPod. Not any old iPod. It has to hold about a billion songs and play videos, too. Nothing but the best for Barbie, and we all know she'll get it. Her friend Sierra is asking for a snowboard. That's not cheap, either, so I wouldn't ask for it even if I wanted it. But Sierra's parents are rich, which means she'll be pleasantly NOT surprised to find it under the tree on Christmas morning.

They're lucky. Not because they get what they want, but because they want what they get. A boy I know wants a new basketball. He's—*the next part had been heavily erased and written over*—He's even luckier.

Was Kayla writing about Jordan at this point? Angela wondered. She thought so. He was the only person not named, which was significant, and there was emotion behind all those eraser marks.

Angela frowned and kept reading.

Tyler Jameson is asking for an Xbox. *Tyler was Jordan's best friend, which seemed to offer more proof that she'd segued from the boy she liked to his best friend.* He's always making a list of the games he wants—at $60 apiece. His Christmas isn't going to be cheap. Money. I wish it could buy what I want. I wish I could be satisfied with an iPod or new clothes, or even getting my ears pierced. But I don't care about any of that. I want something Santa can't pull out of a sack. I want a real last name. The kind that came before I did. Not,

"We'll just call her…" I want to know what my name should've been. I want to know who I belong to. I want my father. Then I could ask him why he loved my mother enough to make me but didn't love me enough to stay.

If I knew him, I think even I could be happy with an iPod.

By the time she finished, Angela's throat had constricted and she doubted she could speak. She didn't know what to say, anyway. As tears filled her eyes, she felt Mrs. Bennett's hand close over hers.

"Heart-wrenching, isn't it?" she said softly.

Surprised at the empathy in the teacher's voice, Angela nodded. Evidently Mrs. Bennett wasn't quite as stern as she appeared. But Angela wasn't sure why she'd called her in to read this essay. Angela couldn't give Kayla what she wanted. Kayla's father didn't even know she was alive—and, because of what had happened thirteen years ago, Angela couldn't tell him. This letter only made her feel worse because now she knew that nothing she could buy Kayla for Christmas would make the girl any happier.

"She's a…a deep child," Angela managed to say.

"She understands what really matters."

Angela sensed that Mrs. Bennett had more to say, but the teacher wasn't quite as direct as usual. She seemed to choose her next words carefully. "You've already shared with me the situation that motivated you to take her in. Have you heard from her mother lately?"

"Not for a few months." Angela had had little contact with her friend since Stephanie had turned to prostitution in order to support her drug habit. Angela had tracked her down a number of times and tried to get her off the streets. She'd planned to put her in yet another drug rehab center. But during their last encounter, Stephanie had spent one night with them, stolen all the money out of Angela's purse and disappeared before she and Kayla could get up in the morning. Without so much as a goodbye or an "I love you" for Kayla.

The incident had upset Kayla so much that Angela had decided she didn't want to see Stephanie again. She had to let go of the mother in order to save the daughter. Which was why she was selling her house. She couldn't have Stephanie dropping in on them whenever she felt like it, disrupting Kayla's life. Kayla had refused to come out of her room for nearly three weeks after the last visit.

"You've never mentioned her father," Mrs. Bennett said. "Do you know anything about him?"

"I'm afraid not," Angela lied.

"Do you think a little research might help? Even if the circumstances surrounding Kayla's birth weren't good, the information might assuage the terrible hunger I sense in her through these words—and in some of her other behavior, as well."

Angela sensed that hunger, too. But telling Kayla about her father would start a chain reaction that could disrupt, possibly ruin, a lot of lives. Besides, Angela had promised Kayla's late grandmother—the woman who'd provided a foster home for Angela after her parents died—that she would *never* tell.

"There's no way to find him," she said. "I've tried."

"Recently? Because now that we have the Internet—"

"It was a one-night stand. Her mother

didn't even know his name." Another lie, but Mrs. Bennett seemed to buy it.

"I see." She shook her head. "I'm sorry to hear that."

"It's unfortunate." The whole thing was unfortunate—and only one person was to blame.

"Okay, well, we'll continue to do what we can to make Kayla feel loved, won't we? Thanks for coming in. I hope you both have a wonderful Christmas."

"Same to you," Angela said and stood as if nothing had changed. But a thought she'd had several times in the past was stealing up on her. What if she were to take Kayla back to Virginia City for a visit? It'd been thirteen years. Surely, Matthew Jackson would never guess after so long. It would give Angela a chance to assess the situation, determine where Matt was now, what he was doing—and whether or not there was any chance he might be receptive to such a shocking secret.

"WHEN WILL WE GET THERE?" Kayla asked.

"Sometime tomorrow." Gripping the wheel with one hand, Angela turned down the Christmas music she'd put on as soon as they'd set off and glanced over at the girl who'd come to live with her fifteen months earlier. With long brown hair, wide brown eyes and a spattering of freckles, Kayla wasn't the prettiest girl in the world. She had the knobby-kneed clumsiness often seen with lanky children who were poised for more growth—she was going to be tall, like her father—but Angela had no doubt she'd grow into a beautiful woman. Kayla held herself with a certain grace and dignity that Angela found impressive, considering everything she'd been through.

The girl had spirit. Her mother hadn't broken it. The kids at school hadn't broken it. Even Kayla's wish for something she'd probably never get hadn't broken it.

Angela was going to make sure nothing ever did. "MapQuest said it'd be about fifteen hours. Is that okay?"

"It's great," she replied. "I didn't realize Denver was so far from where you grew up."

Kayla's excitement lessened Angela's anxiety about returning to Virginia City. Maybe their second Christmas together would be everything she'd hoped. It certainly couldn't be worse than the first, when

Stephanie had shown up completely wasted and without a gift for Kayla. "I wish we could drive straight through, but we started too late this morning." Last night they'd stayed up late packing, so they hadn't gotten up as early as Angela would've liked.

Kayla took a rubber tie from her wrist and pulled her thick hair into a ponytail. "We can go as far as possible before we stop, right? I'll help keep you awake. I love long car rides."

Angela smiled. "So do I."

"Is that why we didn't go on a plane?"

"Partly. That and the fact that Virginia City's a very small town. If we'd flown, we would've landed in Reno and then had to rent a car. And since we'll be staying for two weeks, I'd prefer to have my own transportation." Angela liked the flexibility having her car would provide. She and Kayla could head home anytime they wanted, without notifying anyone.

If she found Matt happily married with a few kids, she'd probably do that sooner rather than later.

"What if we run into a storm? Will we have to stop?" Kayla asked.

"That depends. I brought chains, but if it's

snowing too hard, we might want to get a room and wait it out."

Kayla adjusted the seat belt so she could turn toward Angela. "Are you excited to see all your old friends?"

"The few who still live there," Angela said.

"Almost everyone moved away?"

"A lot of us did. Unless you run a restaurant, a store or a hotel—or you're willing to commute twenty-five miles to Reno—it's not easy to make a living in Virginia City."

"So who do you think is still there?"

"Sheila Gilbert, a friend of mine and your mother's from high school, according to last year's Christmas card. Other than that, probably just a few teachers I had when I went to school and some of the older, more established folks."

"What about boys?"

Angela switched lanes to go around a semi. "What about them?"

"Won't you want to visit some of your old boyfriends?"

"I didn't have a lot of boyfriends." When her mother had died eight years after her father, Angela had only been ten years old. She'd gone to live with her aunt Rosemary, until Rosemary had fallen and broken her hip. Then Angela had moved to Virginia City to live with Betty, who was a distant relative of Rosemary's husband and also Kayla's grandmother. From then on, Angela had spent most of her time trying to keep Stephanie, Betty's real daughter, out of trouble. But she didn't add that. Neither did she admit that the one man they probably *would* see was the person who made her the most uneasy. She doubted Kayla's father had moved on, like so many others, because he came from some of the earliest Irish miners to settle in Virginia City and had a lot of family in the area. And, if he'd married Danielle as everyone had expected, he'd have even more reason to stay. Her parents owned one of the nicest hotels in the Comstock region.

Kayla studied her for a moment. "Whoever sees you is going to be impressed."

Angela chuckled. "Why's that?"

"You're still so pretty."

Still? Actually, Angela had bloomed late. She'd been tall, skinny and reserved, a foil for the boisterous and impulsive Stephanie. But at least her acne was gone, she knew how to apply a little makeup and she'd gained fifteen pounds in the places she'd needed it most, so she was no longer flat and shapeless. Overall, Angela was satisfied with her appearance— and grateful to feel comfortable in her own skin. Maybe her years in sales had done that for her. She'd been marketing large office buildings since graduating with a business degree from the University of Colorado at Denver and dealt with a wide variety of people. That experience had endowed her with confidence poor Stephanie had always lacked.

"You dress nice," Kayla was saying, continuing her list of Angela's assets. "And you have a really great car. I *love* this car."

"Fortunately, it's easier to make money in Denver than it is in Virginia City," Angela said.

"Is that why you moved away?"

No, they'd moved because they'd had to leave. In a hurry. "Your nana wanted a change of pace," she said.

"And you were still living with her?"

"I had my senior year to complete. But I would've gone even if I'd already graduated. It was time for college, so I had to go somewhere. And I wanted to help take care of you."

Kayla made a face. "Since my own mother can't do anything."

Angela didn't respond. She never complained about Stephanie, but she didn't overreact if Kayla made an occasional derogatory comment. The girl had a right to her anger. Stephanie had let them all down in the worst possible way. Sometimes Angela couldn't believe that the friend she'd loved like a sister had made the choices she'd made.

They drove in silence for several minutes. Angela was about to turn the music back up when Kayla spoke again.

"Do you think you'll ever get married?"

"Maybe."

"You don't date much." The words sounded almost accusatory.

"I'm too busy with work."

"Most people go out *at night*," she said. "You're usually home by six, remember?"

Angela shrugged. She didn't like leaving Kayla home alone. "I'll meet the right man eventually."

Kayla seemed thoughtful, almost brooding. "What if you find someone, and he doesn't like me?"

"I can't imagine anyone not liking you."

Kayla's attention shifted to the scenery flying past her window. "You've forgotten Barbie and her friends," she said bitterly.

"Shallow, mean girls don't count."

"What about Jordan? He was nicer than everyone else. Until they started teasing him about me." Her tone turned glum. "Now he won't even look at me."

"That could change as you get older."

"Still. I know you feel like you owe Nana for taking you in, but I don't want to be the reason you don't have a life of your own. You're not the one who got pregnant at sixteen."

Angela reached across the seat to squeeze Kayla's hand. "Kayla, I love you. You're a central part of my life, and no one will *ever* change that."

"But don't you wish I had a father who'd come and take me off your hands?"

"No, I don't," she said, and she realized as she spoke that it was true. As difficult as the past year had been, she didn't want to lose Kayla. Kayla was her only family.

CHAPTER TWO

MATTHEW JACKSON SAT with longtime friend and fellow firefighter Lewis McGinness at a table in the bar and restaurant on the first floor of the Old Virginny Hotel. With wooden oak floors, flocked wallpaper, a dark, ornately carved bar and a tin ceiling, the place had been restored to the glory it had known as a saloon in the booming silver era that had once made Virginia City the most important settlement between Denver and San Francisco. There was even a man dressed in nineteenth-century costume playing lively Christmas carols on a piano in the far corner, next to a Christmas tree adorned with paper chains and popcorn strands.

It was all for the benefit of the tourists, of course—a group of whom stood brushing the snow from their coats and marveling over the glass case by the register, which contained a few items originally owned by the famous 1860s soiled dove, Julia C. The display was designed to generate interest in the Bullette Red Light Museum down the street, where folks could see more *intimate* items, as well as some nineteenth-century medical instruments, all for a buck.

It was worth a buck, right?

Matt shook his head. Heaven knew *something* had to stimulate new interest in this town. Cut into the side of a mountain almost two miles above sea level, with its houses and businesses sitting on as much as a forty-percent grade, it wasn't a convenient place to live. Although, at its peak, the town had boasted nearly thirty thousand citizens, it was down to about fifteen hundred and had been struggling since the early 1900s, when the mines had played out. But Matt had never thought of it as desperately hanging on to what once was. It was home, pure and simple. And yet, as the snow piled higher and higher outside, he had to acknowledge that Virginia City had seen better days, even in his lifetime.

In any event, it was turning out to be a long, cold year. After his older brother, Ray, and his wife had pulled up stakes and moved to Reno last October, Matt was beginning to feel a little like a stubborn holdout—which was how he'd begun to view the town. He wasn't experiencing much of the Christmas spirit today, despite the snow, the lights that trimmed the buildings, already twinkling in the storm-darkened sky, the music.

"I should move to Arizona," he said, sipping some of the foam off the top of his beer. "If I lived in the desert, I'd never have to shovel another walk."

McGinness didn't look up. He was too busy settling his giant, bear-like hands around the half-pound burger he'd ordered for lunch. "Good idea."

Matt glanced at him sharply. "Did you just agree with me?"

"Then I'd get your job, right?" he said, a mischievous twinkle in his eyes.

Tipping back his chair, Matt scowled. "You could at least act as if you'd be sorry to see me go. I've been your chief for what, ten years?"

"I'd miss you," he said, but shrugged. "In between spending the extra money I'd be making off my raise, of course."

Matt righted his chair. "Remind me to fire you when we get back."

"Why are you putting it off that long?"

"It's your turn to pay for lunch, remember?"

McGinness swallowed his first bite and managed a grin. "Come on, you're not going anywhere, Chief. This place is in your blood." He took another bite and spoke with his mouth full. "And then there's Kim."

Matt started in on his French dip sandwich. "What does Kim have to do with anything?"

"She keeps your bed warm at night, doesn't she?"

Not anymore. The moment she'd begun talking about marriage, he'd backed off. He wasn't eager to make their relationship permanent, and getting any closer risked a messy breakup. He'd had a couple of messy breakups in his life, enough to know that even one was too many. "I like Kim. She's a nice woman. But there's something missing," he admitted.

"Like your ability to commit?" McGinness stuffed a couple of fries into his mouth.

"You're a regular comedian today, you know that, Lew?" Matt said.

"Just trying to be helpful."

Matt was about to tell him to shut up and

eat when the door opened and a woman stepped into the saloon. She had shiny black hair cut in a style that hit a fraction of an inch below her chin—definitely too sophisticated for these parts—and a smooth, olive complexion. She also had a girl with her, who appeared to be twelve or thirteen years old. But it was the woman who caught his attention. She was *gorgeous,* but that wasn't it. He was pretty confident he recognized her.

He leaned over to get a better look. Sure enough. It'd been thirteen years since he'd seen her, but he was almost positive she was the girl who'd come to live with Stephanie Cunningham when they were in junior high. What was her name? Angela? That was it—Angela Forrester.

"What's the matter?" McGinness asked.

"Nothing." Matt quickly controlled his expression. He didn't want to say anything that might make Lewis gawk at her and draw the woman's attention. Their last exchange hadn't been good. She'd been there the night Stephanie had caused him to lose the only girl he'd ever really loved. He was fairly sure Angela was partly responsible. But he didn't know how she'd participated or why, and the last thing he wanted to do was relive the humiliation and embarrassment. Luckily, Stephanie had moved away only a few weeks after that incident and had never contacted him again.

"Let's go," he said, tossing twenty-five bucks on the table.

McGinness held on to the rest of his hamburger as though he'd rather part with his left hand. "*What?*"

Matt fixed his gaze on his plate before Angela could catch him watching her. "Never mind," he muttered, settling back in his seat. "Just hurry so we can get the hell out of here, okay?"

MEMORIES PELTED ANGELA like the snow blowing thickly outside. She'd missed Virginia City more than she'd realized. Closing her eyes, she took a deep breath, reveling in the familiar scents of food, coffee, pine trees and wet leather. Because of the cold, Denver could smell fresh and clean in winter—but no place smelled as authentically "Old Fashioned Christmas" as Virginia City. Maybe that was because it hadn't changed much since it had been rebuilt after the great fire of 1875. Standing in the largest federally designated historical district in America made Angela feel as if she'd just stepped out of a time machine. She'd gone back into her own history. To Christmas, the way it used to be.

"It's great here, isn't it?" she breathed to Kayla as they crossed to an empty table.

"I like it," Kayla replied, but she kept glancing over to another table, where two firemen were having lunch.

"What is it?" Angela asked above a lively piano rendition of "Deck the Halls."

"That man was staring at you when we walked in."

Angela opened her mouth to say that after so long, chances were slim they'd know each other. But then she caught a better glimpse of him and felt her jaw drop. Surely they couldn't have run into Matthew Jackson the moment they'd pulled into town....

"Do you know him?" Kayla asked, peering closely at her.

Angela had no idea what to say. They'd chosen a table less than fifteen feet from Kayla's father!

"Angie?" she prompted.

Angela found her voice. "Yes, I—I knew

him as a...a guy in high school." Although she had to acknowledge that he'd improved quite a bit. With dark whiskers covering his prominent jaw, and smile lines bracketing his mouth and eyes, he'd matured into a man who appeared rather rough-hewn. And while his sandy-colored hair had darkened, the unusual ice-blue color of his eyes hadn't changed at all.

"He's handsome, isn't he?" Kayla whispered.

He was so handsome Angela almost couldn't stop staring. And it wasn't just his face. He'd put on maybe thirty pounds since graduation, but none of it had gone to his middle. He filled out that uniform to perfection, looking larger than she remembered him, and far more powerful.

Angela tried to gather her wits, but she was suddenly so nervous she was afraid to remain in the same restaurant. *He doesn't know,* she told herself.

But the doubts she'd wrestled with from the beginning crowded in. *What if he guessed? Would he? Could he?*

On the drive over, Angela had convinced herself that the answer to those questions was *no.* Matt had been with Stephanie only that one night, when they were sixteen, and he hadn't really *chosen* to be with her even then. He wouldn't expect a child from one brief encounter, especially a child he'd never heard about. Besides, Stephanie had trouble carrying Kayla and she'd delivered two months early. That alone would make it difficult to figure out the dates.

Which meant it didn't matter that Angela had suddenly shown up with a twelve-year-old girl in tow.

Reassured by her own reasoning, Angela immediately turned to the menu. But, inside, she couldn't help grimacing at the terrible trick Stephanie had played on Matt. Angela felt partially responsible, but once it had happened, there was no way to fix it—other than doing what Stephanie's mother had done. Angela didn't think she could've stopped Stephanie, anyway. She'd never seen a girl so single-mindedly determined to get what she wanted. And what she'd wanted was Matt.

Ironically, she'd also never seen a man, who—before and after that night—had so studiously avoided Stephanie. It was almost as if Matt had sensed the halter she had waiting to slip around his neck....

"Look, here they come," Kayla said.

The words suddenly registered, as well as the accompanying movement behind her and, turning, Angela realized that she also recognized the second man. He was a beefier version of the boy she'd seen with Matt so often in high school—Lewis McGinness, who'd been one of the best linebackers on the football team.

A smile curved his lips as he made his way toward them. Matt followed, seeming much more reluctant.

"Hello," Angela said warmly and stood. A lot depended on her acting ability. She wasn't about to raise suspicion by revealing how shaken she felt. She'd wanted to figure out what kind of man Matt had become before bringing Kayla into direct contact with him. But it was too late; she had to improvise.

"Hey!" Lewis swept her into a hug as if they'd been good friends in high school instead of mere acquaintances. "What brings you back to Virginia City?"

"I'm here for the holidays."

"Where are you staying?"

"We just got into town, so we don't have a room yet. But we'll probably end up at the

Gold Hill Hotel." That was the hotel owned by Danielle's parents, but neither man brought up her name when Angela mentioned it, so she still didn't know if Matt had ended up marrying the girl he'd dated for so long.

"They've made some improvements, but the new Silver Queen is closer," Lewis said.

Angela kept her smile firmly in place, even though she was acutely aware of Matt and his steady gaze. "We'll have to stop by and take a look."

Lewis waved a hand toward Matt, who seemed perfectly satisfied to stand in the background. "You remember Matt, don't you? Or maybe you don't. He went out with Danielle all through school."

Did that mean he wasn't with her now? Angela knew they'd reconciled after the incident at the party, but if their relationship hadn't progressed beyond high school, Stephanie was probably a large part of the reason.

"Hi, Matt." She held out her hand because he made no move to hug her as his friend had.

He shook hands with a definite lack of enthusiasm. "Good to see you again."

I can tell you're thrilled about it, Angela thought sarcastically. But she could understand that. Because of Stephanie, she couldn't possibly evoke pleasant memories for him.

She put a hand on Kayla's shoulder. "This is my daughter, Kayla."

If Kayla was surprised at being introduced like that, she didn't let on. Nodding shyly, she slipped an arm around Angela's waist, acting more relieved than shocked. Angela knew her real mother was an embarrassment to her.

"She's beautiful," Lewis said. "Like her mother."

"Thanks."

"How long will you be staying?"

"A couple of weeks."

He shifted to make room for Matt, but Matt didn't come any closer. "Are you here to see anyone in particular?"

"No, I just wanted to show Kayla the town."

"Where do you live now?"

"In Denver. I'm in real estate." She glanced conspicuously at their uniforms and badges. "And you're both firefighters, I see."

"That's right. Matt here's the chief.

Unless he moves to Arizona." He tossed his friend a meaningful grin. "Then I'm taking over."

"Now you'll never get rid of me," Matt grumbled.

Angela tried not to notice that Matt was even better-looking up close. He'd always been attractive; that, and his popularity, was why Stephanie had wanted him so badly. But the past thirteen years had added a few finishing touches.

"So...is your husband stuck at home, working over the holidays?" Lewis asked.

She shook her head. "I'm not married. You?"

"Tied the knot nine years ago, already got three kids."

"That's wonderful," she said. "And... what about you, Matt?"

"No." He didn't elaborate, but Lewis quickly filled in.

"He's asked quite a few women, but the poor guy can't get anyone to take him."

Lewis wore such a falsely pitying expression, that Kayla laughed out loud and Angela laughed with her.

"How's your friend?" Lewis asked. "What was her name...Stephanie?"

Kayla's arm tightened around her, and Matt's mouth turned grim. "She's fine."

"Where's she living now?"

Angela had no idea. Stephanie partied with one person or another, then drifted on. "In…Colorado."

"What does she do for a living?" Lewis asked.

"Um…she's in sales," Angela said and felt some of the tension leave Kayla as the girl smiled more easily.

Lewis stepped aside to let some people pass through to the exit. "What about Stephanie's mother? She used to babysit me when I was four. Only for a few months, but I still remember her. Does she live in Denver, too?"

The merry music and Christmas atmosphere lost some of its charm. Angela missed Betty, who'd been such a part of this place. This Christmas couldn't be like the ones she used to know. Not without Betty. "No. She had a heart attack and passed away a little over a year ago."

"I'm sorry to hear that."

Angela nodded politely. "It was tough to lose her. She was a nice woman."

There was a respectful pause, then Matt said, "We'd better get back to work."

"See what a slave driver he is?" Lewis teased.

Angela smiled. "It was great to see you again," she told him and meant it. But she wasn't sure she felt the same about Matt.

"Would you and your daughter like to join me and my family for dinner tomorrow night?" Lewis asked. "Matt will be there, too, right, Matt?"

Matt blinked, as if Lewis had caught him off guard and he didn't know how to escape.

"I wouldn't want to impose," Angela said.

"It's no trouble," Lewis insisted. "You might remember my wife. Peggy Sutherland?"

"Was she my age?"

"She's four years younger."

"I can't quite place her," Angela admitted.

"Maybe you'll recognize her when you see her. Anyway, I know she'd love to have you over. She likes to entertain."

By now Angela could see a muscle flexing in Matt's cheek, but if Lewis bothered to notice, he completely disregarded his friend's less than eager response. And, with the goal of getting to know Matt better, Angela chose to do the same. She'd come for a reason, after all. "If you're sure…"

"I'm positive," he said and Angela gave him her cell number so they could make the arrangements.

CHAPTER THREE

As SOON AS THEY were inside the fire station, Matt pulled Lewis to a stop. "What the hell were you doing back there?"

"When?" His friend's eyes widened as if he really was as innocent as he pretended to be.

"At the restaurant!"

"I was doing you a favor, buddy. Didn't you see how beautiful she is?"

He'd been reluctant to acknowledge it. She and Stephanie must have slipped him something that night when they were juniors. He knew it. He'd never wanted Stephanie before. So how had he wound up in bed with her? And at a party, no less? "I'm not coming to dinner."

"Why not?" Lewis said. "I know you're thinking about...*what happened.* I was there that night, too, remember? At least I was there later on, when Danielle walked in and caught you. But that was thirteen years ago. It's time to forgive and forget. Danielle's married and has two kids. And you heard Angela. She's not attached."

"She said she's not married. That doesn't mean she's not attached."

"I got the impression she's not seeing anyone."

Matt stomped into his office. "She doesn't even live here!"

"You might not be living here either, right?" Lewis called to him. "Maybe you'll want to move to Denver instead of Arizona."

Matt cursed under his breath.

"What did you say?"

"Now I'm *really* tempted to fire you."

Lewis stood in the doorway. "You don't want to do that."

"Why not?"

"Because I have your best interests at heart."

Matt slumped into his chair. "Yeah? Even my mother isn't as meddlesome as you are."

"It's time for you to settle down. Being a father is awesome. You're missing out, my friend."

Matt said nothing. He wanted a family. He'd just never cared about anyone the way he'd cared about Danielle.

"Besides, wouldn't you like to know what happened that night?" Lewis went on. "You've always said you don't remember how you ended up in that room with Stephanie."

"I remember bits and pieces, but mostly it's a blur."

"Well, Angela might be able to explain it."

Matt shoved a hand through his hair. Even if she could provide the answers he'd long craved, what was done was done. They couldn't go back and change anything.

Lewis came into the room and leaned on the desk. "So, what do you say?"

Matt still felt a little resentful despite the passing years. But maybe he was overreacting. Angela seemed nice enough as an adult. And there was a slight chance she hadn't been a party to his downfall. Stephanie had certainly never needed her help to try and corner him before.

But every other time, he'd managed to get away. That was the difference!

"Something about Stephanie chilled me to the bone," he said, recalling her overeager smile, the way she brushed up against him at every opportunity, her attention-hungry eyes.

"Angela isn't Stephanie." Lewis bent lower to peer questioningly into his face. "You're not going to back out on me, are you?"

Matt sighed. What the hell. He could survive one dinner. And, as Lewis said, maybe she'd be able to tell him what had really happened so he could finally understand why he'd let Danielle down so badly.

ANGELA SHIFTED NERVOUSLY as she waited next to Kayla on the doorstep of Lewis's wooden A-frame. Set a couple of blocks off C Street, the main business district, it looked like so many of the other homes and businesses in Virginia City—as if it had been built in the late 1800s. It probably had been. But it was recently painted, a muted yellow with white trim, and obviously well-maintained.

She wondered where Matt lived. While they were growing up, his parents had owned a jewelry store called Comstock Silver and Turquoise. She'd watched for it when she and Kayla had driven through the slushy streets—the weather had warmed enough to melt some of the snow that had fallen the day before—but if his parents still had the store, they'd changed the name and the location. An old-fashioned soda shop now resided where the jewelry store had been.

The door opened and a child of about five, with bright red hair and a few freckles, gazed out at her.

"Hello," Angela said.

He continued to stare, but Lewis's voice rose from behind him. "Derek, those are our dinner guests. Invite them in, okay?"

The boy stepped back and opened the door wider just as Lewis crossed the room, obviously intent on making sure his son followed orders. "Hi," he said when he saw them. "I'm glad you could make it."

Dinner smelled like roast turkey. "Thanks for inviting us." She handed Lewis the bottle of wine she'd bought.

He checked the label, smiled as if it met with his approval and asked to take their coats.

Kayla removed her parka and Angela shrugged out of her trench coat. "Thank you. It looks like the weather's clearing up," she commented.

A short, slightly plump woman with hair the same color as the little boy—and lots more freckles—stepped out of the kitchen. "I think we'll have a white Christmas. They're expecting a big storm next week."

She sounded relieved, and Angela guessed that a white Christmas was very important to her. Judging by the many decorations adorning the yard outside and the two Christmas trees—one in the living room and one in the adjoining dining area—she took her holidays seriously.

"Angela, this is my wife, Peggy," Lewis said from the coat closet.

"Nice to meet you." Angela didn't recognize her, but she seemed friendly.

"And this—" he turned and grabbed the boy who'd answered the door, pushing him to the floor in a playful tussle "—is Derek."

The boy squealed and giggled as he struggled to get free, and Lewis finally released him. "He's the youngest of the kids. The older two are with their grandma tonight."

"I wanted to go, too," Derek sulked.

"Grandma takes gingerbread houses to a professional level," Peggy confided, her voice a half whisper. "According to her, he's not old enough."

Hearing this, Derek climbed to his feet and folded his arms. "I can do it!"

"Next year, honey," she promised and returned to the kitchen.

"Have a seat." Lewis motioned to an antique floral couch and matching chair. The living room resembled a Victorian parlor. "Matt isn't here yet, but he'll be along soon. Can I get you a drink?"

Angela accepted a glass of wine; Kayla asked for a soda. "Are Matt's parents still in town?" Angela asked.

"Yeah. But they've upgraded the store. It's now called Virginia City Treasures and Gifts and is located closer to Taylor Street."

Angela opened her mouth to ask about the rest of Matt's family. As much as she believed Betty had done the right thing in taking Stephanie away when she had, the decision affected many more people than just Matt. Would they be angry to learn they had a twelve-year-old granddaughter/niece? In a way, Angela felt they had a right to know. And yet—

A knock interrupted her thoughts. Tensing, she waited for Lewis to answer the door. But he didn't bother. He was setting the table, so he merely barked out, "Come in!"

Matt strode into the room as though he'd

done it a thousand times. And he probably had. He and Lewis had been friends forever.

"Hi, Matt," Peggy called from the kitchen.

"Uncle Matt!" Derek charged him and threw his arms around his knees.

"Whoa, hold on, buddy. Let me set this pie down," Matt said.

The mention of pie brought Peggy hurrying into the living room. "Did you say pie? What kind?"

"What kind do you think?" he teased. "Your favorite."

"Pumpkin?"

"Of course."

She rose up on her toes to give him a hug. He put one arm around her and used the other hand to pat the head of the boy who was squeezing his leg. It was very apparent that he loved these people. But when his eyes met Angela's curious gaze, she could tell those warm feelings didn't extend to *everyone*.

Clearing her throat, she looked away.

"Can I help?" he asked Peggy.

"Yes." She waved him toward the couch. "You can sit down and entertain our guests while I finish up. Lewis will pour you a glass of wine in a minute."

Instinctively, Angela slid over to allow him more room, but it wasn't necessary. He sat at the far end and focused on Kayla.

"How old are you?" he asked.

"Twelve."

His eyebrows went up, and he glanced subtly at Angela. She knew he had to be doing the math, thinking she'd gotten pregnant awfully young. But he didn't say anything. He let Derek climb into his lap and addressed Kayla once again. "Do you like school?"

Angela sat there, rigid with tension, as father and daughter conversed. She'd been crazy to bring Kayla here, she decided. The truth suddenly seemed so obvious. She could see the similarities in their faces— the slightly square shape to Kayla's chin, the high cheekbones, the broad forehead.

But Matt didn't seem at all suspicious. He did seem reluctant to get to know *her,* and even more reluctant to like her, but he had no qualms about Kayla. Of course, she'd said Kayla was her daughter, they'd bumped into each other during a chance meeting, and Lewis had instigated this dinner. It wasn't as if they'd appeared on his doorstep or rung him up out of the blue.

"Not really," Kayla said, answering his question about whether she liked school.

"Why not?"

"It's—" her eyes shifted momentarily to Angela "—it can be tough to fit in."

"For someone as pretty as you?"

She blushed. "Sometimes," she hedged, and Angela guessed she didn't want to appear too pathetic.

"It's tough for everyone sometimes," he said, even though, as far as Angela could remember, it had never been very tough for him. He'd always been one of the most popular boys in school. "What do you want for Christmas?" he asked.

"I'd like to find my dad."

Angela nearly gasped at Kayla's answer. She'd never heard Kayla admit this to anyone else. Until she'd read that essay, she hadn't realized how deeply Kayla missed having a father.

But the words were already out, and there was no mistaking Matt's surprise. "He's not part of your life?"

She shook her head. "No, he—he left us a long time ago. He said he loved my mom, and he promised her they'd be together forever. But then he couldn't handle a crying baby in the house and changing diapers and all that." She wrinkled her nose, basking in Matt's attention. "So he walked out, and left my mom to raise me by herself."

Angela had stiffened at "he left us a long time ago." Kayla had never been told any such thing. This had to be some kind of fantasy, something she figured would be more acceptable than the reality.

Angela wanted to stop her before she could embellish any further but couldn't say anything in front of Matt. A correction might cause Kayla to make some remark that would give them away. *She* was the one who'd lied first, when she'd introduced Kayla as her daughter.

But, in a way, Kayla *was* her daughter now.

"He was older, then?" Matt asked.

"Yeah, uh…a lot older," Kayla said. "We have no idea where he is."

Matt seemed to look more kindly at Angela, probably because he felt sorry for her.

Only sheer will kept Angela from dropping her head into her hands. How had she *expected* this to go?

Certainly not the way it was going…

"I'm sorry to hear that," he said sincerely. "But he's the one who's missing out. You know that, don't you?"

"Time to eat!"

Peggy's announcement brought the conversation to an end, and Angela nearly cried in relief.

MATT COULDN'T BELIEVE that someone had taken advantage of Angela when she was so young. He knew she didn't really have a family; everyone knew that. A foster child wasn't common in Virginia City then or now, so her first appearance at school, when they were in the seventh grade, had caused quite a stir. If he remembered right, Betty Cunningham had given her a home because of some tenuous connection with Angela's family, and Betty hadn't wanted to see her become a ward of the state.

But Betty, a widow herself, had already had her hands full. A bit eccentric, she'd taken in any stray animal that had crossed her path, so she'd had something like three dogs, a couple of cats, some hamsters and a ferret. Matt knew because Stephanie had lured him over to the house once with the promise of showing him the animals. When she'd come on to him, he'd gotten out of there right away, but he'd stayed long enough to see that the situation was unique. Besides caring for all those animals, Betty had had to deal with Stephanie, who'd always been getting into trouble, and Betty herself had been sick a lot.

Suddenly, Matt felt guilty for being so hard on Angela. If Angela had helped to corner him the night he'd had sex with Stephanie, her involvement could only have been in a peripheral way, and it had no doubt been Stephanie's idea. Anyway, Lewis was right—they'd all been so young.

He caught her watching him from across the table and smiled. He hadn't been very friendly to her so far, but it wasn't too late. According to what she'd told him and Lewis, she was in town for two weeks.

He had half a mind to make sure they were the best two weeks she'd ever known.

CHAPTER FOUR

"ANGIE!"

Angela rolled over to find Kayla standing at the side of her bed. "What?" She squinted in the light streaming through the sheers at the hotel window. They'd chosen the Gold Hill Hotel because Angela remembered it so nostalgically from when she'd lived in Virginia City before. "What time is it?"

"It's only eight. But I just talked to Matt. He's off work on Mondays, and he says we want to get an early start."

"Do we have plans with Matt?" she asked, confused. The last thing she recalled was the charming way he'd walked them to their car after the dinner party was over. She'd been terrified he was going to ask her out. Kayla's story had really affected him, and she'd felt his eyes on her all night, had felt him shift closer to her while they'd been watching the movie after dinner. But at the car, he'd kept his hands in his pockets and had merely told them to get a good night's sleep, then had waved as they'd driven off.

She'd thought that would be the end of it, at least for a few days. They'd had an enjoyable night, established a friendship. And now she had a lot to think about. Matt wasn't married, and as far as she could tell, he wasn't involved in a serious relationship. He had a steady job, family in the area, a solid reputation—what appeared from every angle to be a very normal life.

Which made telling him about Kayla a real possibility.

But Angela wasn't sure he'd thank her for the news. His jaw tightened anytime Stephanie was even mentioned. What if he grew angry at the deception and rejected Kayla? Angela couldn't subject Kayla to any more hurt. And Angela was equally afraid of the opposite possibility—what if he decided to take his daughter away from her?

"He wants to know if we'd like to ride the train," Kayla said. "And afterward, he said we could help him pick out his Christmas tree."

Kayla sounded thrilled. She and Matt had

gotten along famously last night. He'd taught her how to play chess while Angela had helped Peggy clean up and had even given her advice about boys. How could Angela say no?

She wouldn't. She'd go and make sure he was everything he seemed to be, and *then* she'd figure out whether or not to tell him.

THE TRAIN RIDE HAD been fun, but short. It was a narrated thirty-five-minute ride through the heart of the Comstock mining region, after which they went to pick out Matt's tree. Angela liked tramping through the snow; it was cold, and she was getting wet, but she felt so *alive*. She tried to convince herself that the flutter of excitement in her stomach was the result of returning home. But she knew it wasn't just Virginia City. Every time she looked at Matt, she felt a sudden warmth.

How long had it been since she'd kissed a man? she wondered as he tied the tree on top of his truck.

Since before Betty's death. Angela hadn't dated in more than a year.

She missed the male-female contact. She also missed the experience of feeling desirable and desiring someone else.

"Are you staring at his butt?" Kayla murmured, her voice scandalized.

Angela hadn't realized that Kayla was watching her. She considered pretending otherwise, but she could tell by the knowing gleam in Kayla's eyes that the girl wouldn't believe it. Regardless of any embarrassment, she decided it was better to acknowledge the truth. "I've never seen a pair of jeans fit quite so well," she said, using her mitten-covered hand to shield her mouth so Matt wouldn't hear her.

Kayla giggled. "You should go out with him."

"No, we leave in two weeks."

"Why not have some fun while we're here?"

"We are having fun—"

"Hey, what are you two talking about?" Finished, Matt faced them with one eyebrow cocked.

It probably wasn't too difficult to tell they'd been talking about *him.* But Angela refused to admit it. "What we want for Christmas?" she said as innocently as possible.

He wiped his sleeve across his forehead as if he'd worked up quite a sweat. She and

Kayla hadn't been much help. They'd chosen the biggest blue spruce they could find and left him to it.

Angela figured firemen liked doing tough stuff. She'd definitely enjoyed seeing him wrestle that tree into submission.

"And what do *you* want?" he asked doubtfully.

Angela shook her head. It was the first time she'd thought about sex in ages, but now that the idea had crossed her mind, she couldn't seem to forget it.

"I'm waiting," he reminded her.

"Um…a purse?"

He scooped up a loosely packed snowball and hit her with it. "Come on, you just made that up."

She scooped up a snowball of her own. "Are you calling me a liar?"

He grinned as if unconcerned about the threat. "I guess I am."

She launched her snowball, but he dodged it easily and hit her with another one. "Are you going to tell me what you were saying to Kayla?"

"No."

"I'm pretty sure I can get you to change your mind," he warned.

"You couldn't torture it out of me," she said and laughed when Kayla managed to hit him while he was distracted.

"That's it," he said and then snowballs began to fly from all three of them. Angela could hear Kayla laughing as she held her own in the battle, and quickly created a small arsenal of snowballs behind a fallen tree. Then, when Kayla drew Matt's fire, Angela took careful aim and *bam!*

He'd taken off his parka while cutting the tree, so when her snowball smacked him in the back of the head, it showered snow down the neck of his thermal T-shirt.

It was more of a direct hit than she'd intended. As he turned toward her, the look on his face told her she was in trouble.

With a frightened squeal, she began running as fast as she could in the knee-deep snow, but it wasn't thirty seconds before he tackled her.

"Tell me you're sorry," he said.

"She thinks you're handsome! She said she likes your butt!" Kayla called and seized the opportunity to save herself by scampering into the truck. Angela heard the click of the locks only seconds after Matt brought her to the ground.

"Thanks a lot, Kayla," she muttered.

He grinned, obviously pleased that Kayla had just handed him total victory, but he didn't let that distract him from his punishment. "Say 'Chief Jackson, I'm terribly sorry to have caused you any discomfort.'"

"No way! You started it!"

"Fine. Then I'm going to finish it." He shoved snow down her jacket, laughing as she bucked and writhed beneath him. But she wasn't feeling nearly as cold as she should've been. And it wasn't long before she could tell that her movements were arousing him, too.

She stopped struggling, but he didn't get up. He smoothed the snow and disheveled hair from her face. "You're beautiful, you know that?" he said passionately.

The fact that she could feel the physical proof of his appreciation didn't seem to bother him. He kept his body snugly against hers, putting pressure on a very sensitive spot—so sensitive that she wished he'd push a little harder.

Her chest rose and fell while she tried to catch her breath. "You never even looked at me when we were younger."

But he hadn't looked at anybody, had he? Except Danielle.

He didn't mention his old girlfriend. "I didn't know what I was missing."

"What do *you* want for Christmas?" she asked. She was grasping for anything to change the subject, to lessen the tension.

His gaze lowered to her lips, and his voice grew slightly rough. "To catch you under the mistletoe."

MATT HELD HIS WINEGLASS loosely in his hands as he lay on the rug, staring at the lights on the tree they'd just decorated. Kayla had done most of the work, but now she was in the other room watching a Christmas program on television. Angela sat a few feet away, petting Sampson, Matt's German shepherd.

As her hand moved over the dog's fur, Matt was dying to scoot closer to her—if only to thread his fingers through hers. But after their encounter in the snow, she'd been acting spooked. Whenever he sat near, she backed away. And yet she'd been responsive when he tackled her. The flush in her cheeks had come from more than just physical exertion. He could tell by her eyes.

Maybe she needed more time before she'd consider a romantic relationship.

She'd be going back to Denver soon, and long-distance relationships weren't easy, but he couldn't help wanting to get to know her better in spite of that. He felt a sort of…excitement he hadn't experienced in years. He hoped she'd stay, hoped they could explore the possibilities. If nothing else, they should make the most of the time she had left.

"What happened to your parents?" he asked.

She'd been sitting with her legs stretched out and crossed at the ankles, leaning back on her hands to admire the tree. But at his question, she changed position so she could reclaim her wine. "My father died when I was two. My mother died when I was ten."

"That's too bad," he said. "How'd it happen?"

"My parents were older when they had me. They'd been told that my father was infertile. And then, at forty-eight, my mother suddenly conceived."

"They must've been thrilled."

Sampson sat up and barked, but when she scratched him behind the ears, he laid his head in her lap. Matt had never seen the dog take to anyone so readily.

"I suppose, in some ways, they were," she

said. "But the fact that it was a little late in life probably tempered their happiness, you know? And two years later, my dad died of cancer. Pneumonia took my mom eight years after that."

"Is it hard to talk about them?" he asked softly.

"No, it's...okay."

He didn't want to bring up any subject that might be painful for her, and yet he wanted to hear the details of her life. "Wasn't there anyone else in your family who could take care of you?"

"No. My parents' brothers and sisters were even older than they were and had finished raising their families. One lived in Belgium. Another was a widow. She tried to take me, but then she fell and broke her hip."

She'd indicated it didn't bother her to talk about her past, but she'd tensed up. He could see it in the way she held her body.

Despite his determination to give her more time, Matt moved toward her.

She watched him warily. But when she finally met his eyes, he saw that she wasn't unaffected by the chemistry between them. He couldn't tell what was holding her back, but he knew it wasn't a lack of interest.

Taking her hand, he began stroking her slim fingers. "So you went to live with Betty."

She stared at the places where he touched her, as if mesmerized by his movements. "She was my aunt's husband's second cousin," she said slowly. "When she heard Aunt Rosemary was going to have to put me up for adoption, she knew it wouldn't be easy to find a good home for a ten-year-old, that I'd probably be bounced around in the foster system until I turned eighteen."

"So she decided to take you in."

"Yes." She shivered as his fingers moved up the inside of her arm. Liking the reaction, he immediately imagined her in his bed, and wanted more. But she was still sending him inconsistent signals. Her body responded eagerly, yet she seemed reluctant.

"Do you like this?" he asked.

She nodded.

"What about this?" Lifting her hand, he caressed the sensitive tips of her fingers with his tongue. Then, one by one, he took each finger into his mouth, gently sucking on it.

She didn't answer. But he heard her quiet gasp. She was breathing faster, too. He was willing to bet her heart was pounding right along with his.

Leaning closer, he brushed his mouth lightly across hers.

Good. Better than good. He was just going back for another pass, hoping to claim one deep, wet kiss. Her daughter was in the other room. He didn't want to make Angela uncomfortable; he only wanted to show her what could happen if she gave in to what she was feeling.

But she pulled away before he could show her much of anything.

Matt frowned. "You're not interested?" he murmured in confusion. Surely he couldn't be that bad at reading her responses. He'd never misjudged a woman's receptivity before.

"It's getting late," she said. "We—we'd better go."

She tried to get up, but he held her fast. "Why are you running from me?"

"I'm not running from you."

"What are you afraid of? Why won't you give me the chance to really know you?"

"I'm not afraid of anything."

"I want to spend some time with you, Angela. I want to *be* with you," he said. "*And* I want to touch you."

"I—" She seemed at a loss. "Matt, listen. This…isn't right."

He scowled. "Are you married?"

"I already told you I'm not."

"Are you committed?"

She tucked her silky hair behind one ear. "No."

"What is it, then?"

"I don't even live here," she said.

"*That's* the reason?"

"Isn't it enough?"

"No. Not if you're feeling what I'm feeling. We have two weeks. Who knows where it could go beyond that? We wouldn't be the first people to try and manage a long-distance relationship."

"I'm not feeling anything," she said quickly. "I—I have too much going on in my life. I can't get involved right now."

She was lying about what she felt. The excuse of a busy life sounded flimsy, too.

He opened his mouth to argue. But then he stopped himself. He'd be stupid to press her. She was in full retreat. Pushing harder would make her run that much faster.

They sat still for several seconds, staring up at the tree. "Okay," he said at last.

"I'm sorry," she whispered.

"Will you do me one favor?"

Her gaze moved over him, as if she were committing every detail to memory. "If I can."

"Tell me what happened that night. With Stephanie."

"It's over, in the past—"

"I want to know," he said stubbornly.

She pulled her legs in close and propped her chin on her knees. "Stephanie was always so...impetuous," she said reluctantly.

"Impetuous?" he echoed. "She was the most sexually aggressive girl I've ever met!"

"She had a terrible crush on you."

"Calling it a crush makes it sound normal," he muttered. "It was more like an obsession."

"I know. I tried to get her to leave you alone. So did her mother. She wouldn't listen. She never listened—to *anyone*."

The bits and pieces he could recall began to filter through his mind. "I remember seeing her at the party when I arrived," he said. "You were there, too. She asked me to dance, followed me around. The typical stuff. I was annoyed, but not too worried, you know?"

"Yes."

"It was Danielle's mother's birthday," he explained. "She'd gone out to dinner with her parents and was supposed to meet me later. I can still hear the music, see the people. Someone offered me a beer, but I knew I'd be driving her home that night and said no."

"Is that all you remember?" she prompted when he stopped.

"No. I remember the way Stephanie was touching me, my eagerness to let her. What doesn't make sense is *why* I did what I did. Things got out of control, and I didn't seem to care. Then, in the middle of everything, I'm lying naked on the bed, and Danielle's staring down at me, screaming and crying. Stephanie's there, too, holding the sheets to her bare chest and smiling smugly, as if she'd *wanted* us to be caught."

"I'm sure she did. That would've suited her purpose."

How manipulative was that? He shook his head in disgust. "She told Danielle I'd just *made love* to her, when, regardless of what happened, there was no love involved, and she knew it." He winced at the memory of Danielle vomiting afterward.

"Anyway, I couldn't deny it," he went on, embarrassed all over again. "I really had... you know. But, for the life of me, I can't figure out why I didn't stop. I would never have hurt Danielle that way. I'd had plenty of opportunities to be with Stephanie, if that was what I wanted."

"Did you eat any brownies?"

"Is that where it was?" he asked.

Angela nodded.

"What was it, exactly?"

"Betty's sleeping pills."

"*Sleeping* pills?"

"They were strong. Because of her aches and pains, the doctor prescribed some sedatives. Stephanie simply stole a few from the medicine cabinet and mixed them in when she frosted a couple of the brownies she brought to the party."

"The ones she made for me."

"Yes."

He considered Angela for several long moments. He was relieved to finally have his suspicions confirmed, to know he really wasn't the callous jerk everyone had thought he was.

But that raised another question, one that seemed far more important now than it ever had before. "Did you know what she was planning before you went to the party? Did you help her?"

"No. I only knew that she had hopes of getting with you. She said you'd 'be hers' by morning. But she always talked like that. I didn't realize, until she admitted it the next day, that she'd drugged you."

He sighed. "I'm just glad she didn't get pregnant. Can you imagine? It would've ruined my life."

She said nothing.

"Angela?"

"That would have been terrible," she said quietly.

He chuckled without mirth. "I don't know many guys who've had to worry about being seduced against their will, especially at sixteen. Do you?"

"Stephanie was determined. When she wanted something, she stopped at nothing to have it."

He studied her carefully, wondering why she was keeping him at arm's length. "What about you?" he asked.

"What about me?"

"What do you do when you want something?"

She gazed up at the tree. "I try to think about how it'll affect others."

He knew her answer was significant. He just didn't know in what way.

CHAPTER FIVE

"So...DO YOU LIKE HIM?" As soon as they reached their room, Kayla sat cross-legged on the end of Angela's bed and smiled eagerly, obviously expecting a girl-to-girl chat.

"He's nice," Angela replied, trying not to sound too enthusiastic.

"Just *nice?*"

Angela stepped into the bathroom to undress. "No, he's cute, too."

"Oh, my gosh!" she called back. "Cute? He's like...Jake Gyllenhaal. Are you blind? I sat in there watching stupid television shows so you could be alone, and now you're telling me he's *cute?*"

"When I said he had a nice butt, you told on me," Angela accused, trying to put Kayla on the defensive.

But when Angela emerged in her pajamas, she found Kayla stretched out on the bed, grinning unrepentantly. "Yeah, but he liked hearing it. He hasn't been able to keep his eyes off you since."

Angela's head hurt from all the conflicting emotions. When she'd first decided to return to Virginia City, she'd expected to find Matt happily married with a few kids. She couldn't show up on a man's doorstep, a man who had a wife and children, and tell him he had another daughter he'd never even heard about. Not when the child had been conceived the way Kayla had. He wasn't responsible for what had happened, so how could she justify disrupting his life and the lives of those he loved? Knowing she couldn't do that had made her feel safe. She'd come here to put to rest the unsettling "what if" scenarios that had plagued her, even before she'd read Kayla's essay. She'd wanted to validate the decisions that had been made in the past and gather more strength and determination to continue with things as they were.

Now she didn't know what to do. She'd never bargained on Matt's being single. Neither had she guessed that she'd be so attracted to him. Their interest in each other confused an already difficult issue. But with or without Kayla, she saw little chance that what they felt would ever turn into a committed, long-term relationship. They were both single at twenty-nine. That had to say something about them. Her life and her business were in Denver; his were here in Virginia City.

She wouldn't tell him, she decided. Not yet. She didn't know him well enough. Besides, as much as Kayla thought she wanted a father, Angela wasn't sure the sudden upheaval and total change of situation would be good for her.

And yet...she felt guilty for keeping the secret. How could she deny Kayla the chance to know the man who'd fathered her? Especially when Angela had discovered it was Kayla's deepest desire?

Smothering a sigh, Angela sat next to Kayla on the bed. *What would be best for this girl?* She'd promised Betty she'd never tell. But Betty had only been trying to right Stephanie's wrong, to make sure others wouldn't be hurt by it. When Betty had asked Angela for that promise, she'd been assuming Matt wouldn't *want* to know he had a daughter.

Now, Angela wasn't so sure. "What do

you think of him?" she asked and tried to listen beyond the actual words.

"I think he's great," Kayla said. "Perfect."

"In what ways?" she prodded.

"He listens when we talk. He's patient and funny."

"We've only known him a couple of days," Angela said.

"That doesn't matter. He won't change."

Angela pulled Kayla into an embrace. She thought the same thing. But she had to be positive. And, as she stroked the girl's hair, she couldn't help wondering—was Matt ready for the shock of his life?

CHRISTMAS WAS IN FOUR DAYS and Matt hadn't bought a single present. He was reminded of that when his mother called him at work the following morning.

"You're coming to the gift exchange, right?" she said.

He rolled away from his desk and locked his hands behind his head, stretching his aching back. He'd been doing paperwork since he'd arrived at seven, and it was nearly noon. "Why aren't we having the party on Christmas Eve?" he asked.

"Because your uncle Jim's leaving for

New York. He and Don have wanted to see the city for years, and that's their Christmas present to each other."

"I see. So…" Matt rummaged through the stacks of papers on his desk to unearth his calendar. "When is it again?"

"Tomorrow night. At seven."

"Okay. I'll be there." He jotted it down and started to hang up, but his mother was still talking.

"And do not have that friend of yours make Grandma any more eggnog," she said.

He lifted the phone back to his ear. "Why not? She likes it."

"It gives her gas."

"Then why does she ask me for it?"

"The taste. Haven't you ever liked something that wasn't good for you?"

He was beginning to wonder if Angela fit into that category.

"You know how stubborn she is," his mom added.

"What else should I get her?"

"What about one of those firemen calendars you and the other guys posed for?" It had been a local effort to raise money for burn victims.

"You're joking, right? What would an

eighty-year-old woman want with pictures of me and a bunch of other half-naked firemen?"

"She likes Lewis."

"*Lewis?*"

"She says you're never too old to pretend."

He kneaded his forehead. "Mom, that's not creating an appealing mental picture."

"You're not the only one who likes sex in this family," she said. "Your father and I—"

"Mom! Stop!"

"Have always been crazy for each other," she finished. "Oh, and bring some calendars for your aunt. She wants to give a few of them away."

"I've got to go," he said.

"When are you planning to do your shopping?"

He scowled. "How do you know I haven't done it already?"

"Because you always wait till the last minute. You need a wife, Matthew."

"You've been saying that for years."

"And you've been ignoring me for just as long. You think I want to die without grandkids?"

He rolled his eyes. "You're barely fifty-five."

"And I feel every year of it. Your brother and his wife say they don't want children. Can you imagine that? You're my one hope, and you haven't had a steady girlfriend in years." She hung up, sounding thoroughly disgusted but, after a few seconds, Matt called her back.

"Can I bring a couple of people to the party?"

"Lewis and his family?"

"No. A woman and her daughter."

There was an intrigued silence. "You've never brought a woman to the gift exchange before. Do I know her?"

"She used to go to school with me. Now she lives in Denver."

"*Really...* Would she ever consider moving here?"

"I don't know."

"Has she seen the calendar?"

He waved as one of the guys called out to him from his open door. "What does that have to do with anything?"

"Bring an extra one just in case," she said and disconnected.

PULLING HER MINISKIRT down as far as it could go—to mollify Angela's nosy neighbors, two of whom were staring out their windows at her—Stephanie promised the cab driver that she'd pay him in a second and hurried up the walk. The house looked empty, and there was a For Sale sign in front, but Stephanie could see that the furniture was still in the living room. Angela might be planning to move, but she hadn't done it yet.

Her barely there sweater was more effective at attracting customers than keeping her warm, but she wrapped it around herself as well as she could and knocked on the door. Meanwhile, she could feel the neighbors' eyes boring holes in her back. A cab in this exclusive area drew too much attention. She should've had the driver drop her at the corner so she could walk, but he probably wouldn't have done it anyway. He didn't want to let her too far out of his sight; she hadn't paid him yet.

No one came to the door. "She's got my kid. But do you think she'd give me a number or tell me where the hell they're at?" she grumbled. She knew she'd made Angela mad the last time they'd seen each other. After that, her friend's numbers had all changed without warning. But Stephanie hadn't wanted the help Angela had offered. She could live her own life, thank you very much.

Glancing at the waiting taxi, she waved to reassure him and hurried around to the gate. She felt jittery, shaky, ill—and she knew it wasn't related to the bronchitis she'd had for over a week. She needed some junk before her symptoms got worse. But if she couldn't get inside the damn house, how was she going to get any money?

The back door was locked as tight as the front. Stephanie could see a single light shining in the living room, the typical "sorry, we're not home but don't want you to know it" light, and considered breaking a window. She didn't have any choice, did she? She had to get in, find a few bucks and get out. Before the neighbors could stop her.

Her mind was fixated on the quarters and dimes Angie threw in a big jar on a shelf in her closet. There had to be thirty, forty bucks in there.

Angie didn't need it. She never used it. Stephanie knew that was all it would take to carry her through the night. It'd be different if she'd been able to work. But what man wanted to pay for a woman with a raging fever and a hacking cough?

Finding a rock in the planter area next to the French doors, she bent to pick it up. But her hand was shaking so badly she could hardly lift it, and by the time she'd managed, the man from next door was standing less than ten feet away.

"Can I help you, miss?"

She dropped the rock and ducked her head so he couldn't see the black eye she'd sustained from a particularly rough customer four days earlier. "Angie, she—she's my friend. She said I could borrow forty bucks, to—to come on over and get it. But I—I got a cab waiting out front. And she's not here."

"She told you to come over."

It wasn't a question. He was looking down his nose at her, like all the other rich bastards in this neighborhood.

"That's what I said, isn't it?" She knew her voice had grown belligerent, but she couldn't seem to control it any more than she could control the shaking. She couldn't think straight. The terrible need inside her was eating her up....

"But that couldn't possibly be true," he replied. "As you can see, the house is closed up. She's gone for the holidays."

Gone for the holidays? Angie never went anywhere for the holidays.

"She—she said she'd give me forty bucks," Stephanie insisted.

"I think maybe you should seek a shelter and some professional help," he said.

Finally, she faced him squarely. "Listen, buddy, I—I'll give you a blow job right here for twenty bucks," she whispered. "I'll do anything else you want for forty."

He didn't take her up on her offer. He shook his head sadly, reached into his wallet and gave her the money.

ANGELA WAS PRETTY SURE that attending Matt's family's Christmas party was not a good idea. She would've said no—except that he'd asked Kayla first. And Kayla had, of course, immediately accepted. Kayla was playing cupid. She liked being around Matt. A lot.

"Matt told us you two went to school together," Ben, Matt's father, said after they'd been ushered in and offered a drink. He was doing his best to make her feel comfortable.

Angela glanced over at Matt, who stood by the punch bowl. He was talking to his brother and sister-in-law, who'd come from Reno, and a couple of uncles or cousins. Angela had been introduced to everyone, but Matt had such a big family, she was starting to lose track of who they were and how they all fit in. "That's right. I lived with Betty Cunningham."

Matt's dad was an older version of Matt, except there was gray mixed in with his dark blond hair, and he had brown eyes. Matt's mother was almost as tall as his father, and significantly overweight, but she was jovial and warm.

"Betty was a wonderful person," Ben said. "Loved jewelry. Came down to the store often."

Angela liked the rustic log home Matt's father had built. A mile or so from town, it was cut into Mount Davidson, like the other homes and businesses in the area, and smelled of the fire crackling in the hearth. Scrupulously clean and well-decorated in rustic browns and reds, it had a wall of windows in front. The Christmas tree stood before the windows, reaching all the way to the center beam of the polished wooden ceiling, its lights reflecting in the glass. Angela guessed that in the daytime, the

Jacksons had a lovely view of the Como Mountains.

"I miss her," she admitted. Somehow, the hustle and bustle of the party and the easy camaraderie between all these people only added to Angela's sense of isolation.

"Your daughter is such a nice girl." Sherry, Matt's mother, joined them now that she'd finished whatever errand had sent her scurrying to the kitchen with Kayla as soon as she and Angela had arrived.

"Thank you."

"I've got her decorating cookies with my sister's kids," she confided. "She's a natural."

"I'm sure she'll like that." Angela caught Matt watching her. She smiled as if she were having a good time, but she wasn't. She didn't want to be here. This showed her what Kayla could have—without her.

"WHAT'S WRONG?" Matt asked.

Angela had left the party and stepped onto the extensive deck that wrapped around his parents' home. A chill wind was blowing—possibly the beginning of the storm Peggy McGinness had predicted—but there was a full moon and when he came up next to her, he could see the snow glistening far below. It was beautiful. But not half as beautiful as the woman staring forlornly down at it.

She glanced over at him. "Nothing, I just... needed some fresh air."

"Are you overwhelmed by the crowd?"

"No," she said, but when she met his knowing gaze, she instantly recanted. "Yes."

He chuckled with her. "You get used to the chaos."

"They're great. You're very lucky."

He knew he shouldn't touch her. He'd promised himself he'd take the relationship more slowly, so she wouldn't rebuff him again. But she looked so lost standing there, he couldn't help trying to comfort her, include her. Moving behind her, he gripped the wooden railing, penning her between his arms. He was hoping she'd lean back and let him hold her, but she didn't. "They really like Kayla," he said.

She had a strange expression on her face when she twisted to peer up at him.

"Angela?"

She studied him for a moment, then seemed to relax. "She likes them, too. She—she's never had anything like this."

He slipped his arms around her, pulling her into full contact with him. He wanted to shelter her from the cold, close the emotional distance she kept putting between them as easily as he could close the physical one. If she'd let him… "Neither have you."

She didn't answer.

Lifting her hair, he pressed his lips to her neck. "Why not open up? Give it a try?" he asked softly.

"Matt, I—" He stiffened, afraid she was going to pull away again. "I have something to tell you."

The tone of her voice didn't sound promising. "What's that?"

"It's about that night, with Stephanie."

He could tell by how rigid she'd gone that this wouldn't be good. Could she have warned him and hadn't? He no longer cared. That was thirteen years ago, and Stephanie had probably dragged her into it. He wasn't going to allow what had happened then ruin what could happen now. "I don't want to talk about that night," he said. "As far as I'm concerned it never took place."

"But Stephanie—"

"Doesn't exist."

"Is that what you want?" she asked fervently. "To forget? To live your life just as it is?"

"This is what I want," he responded and, keeping their backs to the house in case anyone glanced out, he slid his hand up her smooth, flat stomach.

CHAPTER SIX

ANGELA KNEW BETTER than to let their relationship get physical. Matt claimed he didn't care about what had happened thirteen years ago, but he didn't understand. There was a living, breathing person as a result of that night. Surely, he'd want to know.

Or maybe not. Maybe he liked his life exactly as it was. That was what he'd implied.

But now wasn't the time to dwell on her worries. His fingers were lightly caressing one breast through the thin fabric of her bra, sending shock waves of pleasure cascading through her.

"Matt," she murmured, still torn. Her conscience demanded she stop him, but her body begged her to close her eyes and forget. She'd tried to say his name in a commanding tone—but it came out choked and eager, and she could feel how deeply it affected him.

Pulling her along the railing to a set of stairs, he led her down to a small guest room. Set off from the rest of the house, it had a bed and its own bath.

"Let me see you," he whispered as he shut and locked the door behind them.

In the house above, they could hear Christmas music, laughter, the tramping of feet. But it seemed far removed from them. Angela imagined Kayla grinning from ear to ear, licking frosting off her fingers. For the moment, everyone was happy. There was no need to ruin the party by blurting out the truth *or* to deny themselves these few stolen minutes. What would that really change?

Slowly, Angela slipped her red sweater over her head, watching carefully for Matt's reaction as it dropped to the floor—and was gratified when his eyes darkened and his jaw sagged.

"God, you're more beautiful than I imagined." Bending his head, he cupped her breasts, kissing the swell of one, then the other.

Angela let her head fall back. She

wouldn't think, she told herself. Not about Denver or Virginia City. Not about the past or the future. She'd only *feel*—the feverish excitement building inside them; his deft hands unhooking her bra and sliding around to touch her; his warm, wet mouth closing over the tip of one breast; his muscular body pressing her into the mattress.

MATT COULDN'T BELIEVE he'd brought Angela into his old bedroom right in the middle of his parents' Christmas party. He'd meant to kiss her, to catch a tantalizing glimpse of her body, to touch her briefly. But the situation was quickly spiraling out of control. And he couldn't stop it for fear she'd never let him have another chance. His craving was too great. He had to feel her body's quivering responses, acquaint himself with all the little things that made her moan and writhe and cry out.

He hoped to make this as memorable as possible for her, but he didn't dare take it slow. There wasn't time. He didn't want to embarrass her by being gone so long someone would come looking for them. And the way she was tugging impatiently at his clothes told him she was as frantic as he was.

Once they were undressed, he pulled her down on the bed with him and pinned her arms over her head while he rolled on the condom he kept in his wallet.

She watched him with heavy-lidded eyes, her lips wet and slightly parted. But the gentle kiss he meant to give her quickly turned savage. Soon he was driving into her with powerful, rapid strokes. Minutes later, they were both damp with sweat and gasping for breath. And just when he thought he was too far gone to hold back any longer, it happened. She groaned, met his gaze as if he'd given her the most wonderful gift in the world, and shuddered.

He was only half a second behind her.

STEPHANIE LAY ON THE rumpled bed of the cheap hotel room staring bleary-eyed at the television. She could smell urine and perspiration, but it didn't bother her. She squinted, trying to decide if she was actually watching a program. It didn't matter. The flicker itself was fascinating, especially when her mind was floating so freely around the room. Spinning, moving, gliding...

"Hey, get up, bitch."

Slowly, she turned her head and blinked.

A man's fuzzy shape appeared. Jaydog? "Hey, Jaydog," she said, the syllables running together.

She tried to make her gaping mouth form a smile, but he didn't seem happy with her greeting. A sharp pain suddenly dimmed her euphoria. Had he kicked her?

He was *still* kicking her. And screaming. He wanted her to do something. He wanted her to get out.

Climbing to her feet, she swayed unsteadily as she walked, heading for an opening that was blinding in its brightness. That had to be the door. She misjudged the distance and ran into a corner, causing an additional glancing blow to her shoulder. But then she was outside and the door slammed behind her.

She didn't know how long she stood there before she noticed that she wasn't wearing any clothes.

HE'D MADE A MISTAKE. Matt realized that almost right away. He'd expected his encounter with Angela to bring them closer, to put an end to her cautious reserve.

But after they rejoined the party, she left his side as quickly as she could. He found his gaze trailing after her wherever she went, hoping for a smile or some reassurance that what they'd done was okay—but he got nothing. She wouldn't even look at him. And if there was any accidental contact, she'd recoil.

What was going on? What they'd shared had been a great deal more than he'd expected. Especially so early in their relationship. But she was leaving in a week. It wasn't as if they had months or years stretching out before them. Even if they maintained a relationship, they wouldn't get to see each other very often. Besides, maybe he'd initiated the contact, but her surprising response had been the match that ignited the powder keg. The encounter had been completely spontaneous. Real. Raw.

He couldn't regret it.

Yet she was even less open to him now than she'd been before.

What had he done wrong? He supposed he shouldn't have taken things so far. But he hadn't *planned* for it to happen—not here, anyway.

He wasn't sure when he should've stopped. Angela had never indicated that she'd wanted him to. She'd acted as if she'd been starved for human touch, love.

He'd wanted to give her both.

He took a seat across the room from her and her daughter as his mother started handing out presents. Angela and Kayla sat with polite smiles fixed on their faces—outsiders looking in, enjoying everyone else's gifts and excitement without hoping for anything themselves.

He glanced over, but Angela avoided meeting his eyes. Again.

Maybe she'd been so hurt in the past that she was scared to let down her guard, he decided. She must've had a lonely childhood, after losing both parents and then living like a guest in someone else's house.

Then there was Stephanie. He couldn't even begin to imagine what dealing with her on a daily basis must've been like. Even as an adult Angela seemed to live a pretty solitary life—just her and Kayla. They were both engaging and polite, and he sensed that they wanted closer relationships than they had but didn't know how to reach out because they had no trust.

He remembered Kayla's story about her father. *So he walked out, and left my mom to raise me by herself. We don't even know where he is.*

The bastard had caused some deep scars. "Are you going to open it?"

Matt blinked and focused on his sister-in-law, who'd just shoved a present into his lap.

"Sure," he said, and unwrapped a bottle of his favorite cologne.

"This is great. I was getting low." He gave her a hug, then waited for the process to continue around the circle until it was Angela's and Kayla's turn.

His uncle, who was sitting next to him, received a basket of salami and cheese. Matt's father acted excited over a new hand drill.

At first, Grandma had tried to boycott the gift exchange because his mother had put a ban on the special eggnog Matt usually provided. But then she relented, opened his brother's gift, which was a box of chocolate-covered cherries and, with a spiteful glare for his mother, stuffed three in her mouth at once.

"Wow. You go, Grandma," Ray said, sitting taller for Matt's benefit. "I guess I'm your new favorite grandson, huh?"

Matt shot his mother a look that said, "Next year I'm bringing the eggnog." But he didn't bother to wait for her response. It was Kayla's turn to open her gift, and he didn't want to miss it.

"This is for me?" she asked in surprise when his aunt dug the present out from those that remained.

His mother checked the tag. "Yep. From Matt."

Kayla smiled shyly at him and tore away the wrapping. When she reached the plush blue box inside, she sent him another questioning glance, then snapped open the lid.

Her smile spread across her whole face. "It's a gold locket," she breathed. "I love it!"

Her response filled some of the hollowness Matt had been feeling since he'd left the bedroom downstairs. Especially when she hurried across the room to hug him. Her little arms felt so thin and fragile, as fragile as he imagined her heart must be.

"I'm glad you like it," he said.

She immediately returned to her mother so Angela could help her put it on, but Sherry insisted they let someone else do that so Angela could open her gift.

Angela's eyes flew wide when Sherry set a box in her lap, a box that was much, much bigger than Kayla's. "I'm sorry. I—I didn't bring any gifts," she said self-consciously.

Matt shrugged. "I didn't tell you it was a gift exchange."

She cleared her throat. "You should have."

He hadn't wanted her to feel obligated to go out and buy a bunch of presents. He'd just wanted her to come. "It's fine." Hadn't anyone ever given her a gift she could accept without feeling the obligation to respond in kind?

Probably not. Typically, only parents and grandparents gave gifts like that.

Matt's mother huddled closer to Angela. "Let's see what it is."

"Yeah, open it," Kayla chimed in, her locket now securely fastened around her neck.

Angela unwrapped the box and pulled out the quilt Matt had found in one of the gift shops. Handmade by a local woman, it showed nine historically significant structures in Virginia City—the First Presbyterian Church on C Street, Mackay Mansion on D Street, Piper's Opera House at B and Union, the Fourth Ward School on C, St. Mary's in the Mountains, Storey County Courthouse, the *Territorial Enterprise* Museum, where Mark Twain had begun his career, and the Liberty Engine Company No. 1 State Fireman Museum. In the Fireman square, he'd had the maker stitch *Love, Matt,* along the edge.

"It's beautiful!" Angela exclaimed.

He could tell she really liked it. "I thought it might give you something to remember us by."

"Come on, Matt. Who could forget you?" his brother teased.

"She won't forget you," his mother announced and slapped a square flat present in her lap.

Matt immediately recognized the size and shape, and groaned. "I left those at home. On purpose. How did you get—"

"I have my own stash," she said triumphantly.

Sure enough, it was a copy of the calendar.

"He's May and November," his aunt informed Angela, and just about ripped it out of her hands so she could turn to the right months. "See? Isn't he gorgeous? He's my nephew, but I gotta tell ya, he's the hottest one in there."

He rubbed a hand over his face. "Come on, Aunt Margaret."

His sister-in-law laughed and pointed. "I never would've believed it possible, but I think you're embarrassing him."

Matt scowled. "Why would I be embarrassed? I only did it to help the burn victims."

"Honey, that thing's started more fires than you'll ever put out," his aunt teased.

The whole family had a good laugh at his expense. But Matt didn't mind too much. Not when Angela finally looked up from the calendar and he saw the heat in her eyes.

Maybe she was trying not to acknowledge what she felt. But whatever had caused the frenzy downstairs wasn't gone. Not by a long shot.

CHAPTER SEVEN

SHEILA GILBERT LOOKED much the same as she had in high school. Barely over five feet tall, with shoulder-length blond hair, blue eyes and a curvaceous figure, she'd gained a smoker's voice and somehow lost her ready smile—but those appeared to be the only changes.

"It's wonderful to see you again," Angela said as she and Kayla led the way to a table at the Silver Dollar Café, where Sheila had suggested they meet. A mom-and-pop place that had opened since Angela had left town, the restaurant was located across the street from Matt's parents' jewelry store. Angela had noticed that little detail the moment they'd driven up. Every few seconds, she found her attention drifting to the window— just in case she spotted a member of his family on the street outside. She'd liked the Jacksons. She'd liked them all—

"When did you get in?" Sheila asked.

Angela forced herself to focus. "Last Sunday."

"What brings you back?"

She shrugged as the waitress delivered their water, and Sheila ordered coffee. "I missed it, wanted to see the town," she said when the waitress had hurried away.

"You missed *this* place?" Sheila raised a skeptical eyebrow. "You're kidding, right?"

Kayla's nose appeared above the top of her menu. "You don't like it here, Sheila?"

"What's to like?" she asked.

"Everything," Kayla replied earnestly. "The mountains and the trees and the buildings. And Matt, and his parents and cousins. And his funny grandma."

Obviously, Kayla liked them, too.

"Matt?" Sheila turned to Angela expectantly.

"Matthew Jackson," she said. "We ran into him the first day we got here."

Sheila released a low whistle. "Now I understand. If you've seen Matt, you've seen the very best Virginia City has to offer."

Kayla proudly lifted her locket. "He gave me this at the Christmas party last night."

Sheila held it in her own hand for a

moment. "Very nice." She grinned wryly. "See? That's my problem. He's never given me a locket."

"But you like him," Angela said.

"Who doesn't?" Her voice grew dreamy. "He's a tough catch, so be forewarned. But maybe you're better at big-game hunting than I am. Anyway, he's nice, sexy and brave. He keeps us all safe while looking like a dream in that uniform." She leaned forward. "And have you seen the calendar? I have May permanently taped to my ceiling. The mere sight of that picture makes me—"

Angela cleared her throat.

Sheila's eyes darted toward Kayla. "—makes me proud of our local firemen," she finished. But her smile said what she hadn't been able to say. And Angela completely understood. After Kayla had gone to sleep last night, Angela had sat up staring at the picture that featured Matt with a fire hose slung over one muscular shoulder. He was wearing nothing but a fireman's hat and a pair of pants slung so low on his narrow hips that they revealed the line of hair descending from his navel—the line of hair she'd seen for herself last night, along with what the picture *didn't* show.

The memory of his hands on her body, of his body joining perfectly with hers, played in her mind again.

She pinched the bridge of her nose, hoping to stem the tide of mortification, arousal and embarrassment rising to her face. When he'd brought her home, he'd asked her to call him after she got settled in the room, had murmured that he wanted to talk to her about what had happened between them. She'd mumbled something noncommittal, thanked him for the quilt and turned away before he could give her even a peck on the cheek. But she hadn't been able to make herself dial his number. She felt too guilty for taking advantage of his ignorance where Kayla was concerned, knew it would make him hate her when he found out.

When *he found out*...

Now it was only a matter of time, wasn't it? Because she'd already fallen in love with him and every member of his family. And if Kayla had the chance to be part of them, of what they had, Angela wouldn't let anything stand in the way—least of all herself.

Instinctively, she reached across the table to take Kayla's hand.

"What is it, Angie?" she asked, the question in her voice telling Angela she was squeezing a little too hard.

She *had* to do it, right? She had to tell for Kayla's sake.

The lump in Angela's throat made it difficult to speak. "Nothing. I just—I love you," she said.

Kayla smiled sweetly as Sheila looked on. "I love you, too. I'm so glad you brought me here."

A crushing pain made it difficult to breathe. Letting go, Angela tried to smile. "Me, too," she said, then hid behind her menu because Sheila was watching her strangely, and she knew she'd start crying if she didn't.

God, it's going to be tough to give you up, she thought.

STEPHANIE'S HEAD POUNDED as the voices of the other people droned on and on. She was in a shelter, she realized slowly, lying on a mattress, gazing at the cavernous ceiling. She didn't know how long she'd been there or who had brought her in. But she could tell they'd given her something to help her deal with the spasms that racked her body. She could also tell it wasn't enough.

Getting up, she started for the door. She wanted to go back. Jaydog would fix her up. He always did. For a few tricks, he'd get her exactly what she needed.

A woman wearing nurse's scrubs caught hold of her arm before she could reach freedom. "Miss, I don't think you want to go out there. The help you need is right here."

"You don't have what I need," she argued.

"It isn't easy, but you can do it."

"Let me go." She tried to jerk away, but the woman's grip only tightened.

"Listen to me," the woman said, her voice low, harsh. "Is this the kind of life you want? Look at yourself!" She handed her a mirror, and Stephanie almost didn't recognize the face that stared back at her. When had she gotten so gaunt and haggard? So old? And what had happened to her hair? Had someone set fire to it? Or had she set fire to it herself?

"I need some sleep," she insisted. "I— I'll get a haircut. I'm not as bad as you make me sound."

"Do you want to *live?*" the woman asked.

Stephanie blinked at her in surprise. "*What?*"

"If you want to make it another year, give me the number of someone I can call."

Stephanie took a second look at the stranger in the mirror. Who was that person? Where was she going? What had she done?

She had no answers. She had nothing.

"Who can I call?" the woman repeated, more forcefully.

Stephanie didn't have Angela's cell-phone number. Their relationship had become so rocky Angela had changed the number and wouldn't give it to her. But Stephanie did remember the name of the place where Angela worked.

"WHAT'S WRONG?" Lewis asked, poking his head inside Matt's office.

Matt yanked himself out of the lethargic stupor that seemed to swallow him whole every time he stopped moving, and shuffled some papers around. "Nothing, why?"

"You're not yourself today."

Angela hadn't called him last night. She hadn't even squeezed his hand or thrown him a quick smile when they'd parted. She'd made passionate love to him for about ten minutes, then...no real interaction at all. "Thanks," she'd said as he'd dropped them off. "For everything." And then she'd gone and he hadn't heard from her since.

He shouldn't have taken her into that bedroom. She probably thought he didn't respect her. Or that he was only interested in what he could get from her while she was in town. Or…

Hell, he didn't know. He'd never gotten so many mixed signals in his life. He was thoroughly confused.

"So how was the big gift exchange?"

Lewis was still standing in the doorway of his office.

Matt tried to rouse himself again. "Great. Fun. Grandma didn't get her special eggnog, for which she'll never forgive me. But other than that…" Other than that, it had definitely had its high points. Like the moment Angela had frantically stripped off his pants and greedily touched him everywhere, arching into him when he'd first covered her body with his.

She'd wanted to make love, too, hadn't she? Because if that was *no,* how would he ever know *yes?*

"I ran into Ray a few minutes ago," Lewis said.

"Oh, really? Where?" Matt could hear the

flatness in his own voice, but Lewis didn't comment on his lack of enthusiasm.

"At your parents' store. I stopped by to pick up the necklace I bought for Peggy."

"Peg's going to have a nice Christmas."

"Yeah."

"That's good."

Lewis stepped into the room and leaned on the back of one of the chairs. "Anyway, Peg and I plan to invite Kayla to come to Reno with us tonight."

The mention of Kayla instantly raised Matt's level of interest. "What for?"

"We're going to Circus Circus, you know, for the kids. Then we'll be staying over to have a buffet breakfast and do a little shopping. Christmas Eve is the day after tomorrow, so it's pretty much our last chance. I thought I'd let you know in case you wanted to take the opportunity to be alone with Angela."

Matt felt a sudden flicker of hope. Last night, he'd handled her the way he would a house fire—urgently and without finesse. She must've been disappointed. So…what if he brought her some flowers, took her out for a romantic dinner, spent the evening just getting to know her? If she didn't touch him, he wouldn't touch her. Then maybe she'd forgive him, let him start over... This time, he'd take it slower.

But she hadn't called him even after he'd asked her to.

It was too late.

He shook his head. "Thanks, but I'm not going to bother her again. I don't think she wants to see me anymore."

"CAN WE GET IT FOR HIM? Please?" Kayla begged.

Angela didn't have to ask *For who?* After breakfast, when they'd set off to do some Christmas shopping, Kayla had wanted to find a gift for Matt. Angela did, too. She just hadn't expected to find anything quite like this.

"Please say yes," Kayla said.

Angela lifted the sculpture of a fireman carrying a child to safety and read the plaque at the bottom. *Safe from Imminent Danger.*

Tracing a finger lightly over the face of the child, she took in the details—the smile, the rounded cheeks, the pigtails. It was a girl, which struck Angela as very significant.

"Angie?"

Angela blinked and finally answered. "Yes?"

"It's perfect for him, don't you think?"

It *was* perfect. It was also expensive, but his gifts to them hadn't been cheap, and it said everything Angela wanted to say. *Shelter her from harm. Keep her safe. Be a good daddy.*

She could trust a fireman, right?

WHEN HE HEARD ANGELA at the station, asking to see him, Matt couldn't believe it. He'd just decided she didn't want anything to do with him. And now she was here?

Ruben, one of his men, directed her to Matt's office.

Matt rounded the desk as Kayla came hurrying through the door.

"We got you a present," she said breathlessly.

Angela followed, carrying a large square box wrapped in a paper decorated with little Christmas trees.

"You didn't have to get me anything," he said. But since it had brought them to the station, he was damn glad they had.

Kayla clasped her hands in front of her

as if she could scarcely contain the excitement. "Open it!"

He would have, right away. Except Angela's gaze swept over him from head to toe, so hot and hungry it nearly stole his breath. He hadn't made any mistake last night—she wanted him as badly as he wanted her. So what was the problem?

He didn't know, but he'd certainly ask. Because he now understood that his other plan would never have worked. Considering the force of what they were feeling, what they wanted, there was no way they'd be able to let their relationship develop slowly.

"Hi," he said, his eyes locking with hers.

"Hi," she murmured and gave him such a sexy, mysterious smile he got lost in it for a while—until Kayla tugged on his arm.

"Don't you want to see what we got you?"

He doubted it could compare with what Angela had given him last night. Grinning, he took the package, set it on his desk and tore off the paper.

It was a bronze statue of a fireman saving a child.

"Do you like it?" Kayla asked.

He smiled as he stared at it. "I do. Very much. Thank you."

"Now every time you look at it you'll think of us," she said.

He didn't admit it, but he was afraid he couldn't forget them even if he wanted to.

ANGELA REACHED FOR the phone half a dozen times without picking it up. Tonight was the night to tell him. Kayla had gone to Reno with Lewis and his family, so Angela was alone. She could talk to Matt, explain the pregnancy that had resulted from what had happened thirteen years ago and see what he'd like to do about it before she broke the news to Kayla.

Maybe he'd settle for annual or biannual visits. Why not? He wasn't used to having a child. And it wasn't as if Angela needed him for financial support. She did fine on her own. She'd suggest they share Kayla.

But what if he didn't want to share? He didn't seem like the type to have a part-time daughter. He seemed like the kind of man who claimed what belonged to him and took care of his own.

She wiped her sweaty palms on the old jeans she'd pulled on, along with a sweat-shirt. She was scared. But picturing that essay, those question marks that had replaced Kayla's last name, made Angela reach for the handset with enough resolve to get the job done. Kayla Jackson had a nice ring to it. Matt was a father to be proud of.

The phone rang just as Angela touched it. Taking a deep breath, she brought it to her ear. "Hello?"

"I want to see you. Will you come over?"

It was Matt. Of course. She'd known it would be.

Angela bit her lip. Could she really break her promise to Betty? What if he insisted on raising Kayla, and Stephanie managed to get her life together? Would he include her at all?

There were so many variables, so many risks....

"Angela?"

"I'll be there in fifteen minutes," she said and hung up.

CHAPTER EIGHT

STEPHANIE SAT ON HER COT and kept rocking, back and forth, back and forth. It was the only way to deal with the turmoil inside her. The methadone the nurse had given her was curbing her withdrawal symptoms, but nothing could ease her agitation over what she'd just learned.

When the nurse had called Angela's work number, she'd been told that Angela was out of town. Then the nurse had explained that it was an emergency, and some assistant had said Angela had gone to Virginia City for the holidays.

Stephanie rocked faster. Virginia City. Angie had gone home without her. And she'd taken Kayla. After thirteen years.

Why? That was the question. There was nothing left in Virginia City.

Except maybe Matt.

ANGELA COULD SCARCELY breathe as she waited on Matt's front step—and it didn't get any easier once he opened the door.

Dressed in a pair of faded jeans and a blue striped shirt with a white T-shirt underneath, he was fresh from the shower. His hair was still damp and curled around his collar. She thought he looked better than she'd ever seen him. Especially when his lips curved into a crooked smile as his eyes swept over her, telling her that he liked what *he* saw just as much. "Come in."

She couldn't get physical with him, she reminded herself. They both needed to have clear heads, to make a wise decision uninfluenced by peripheral desires. A decision about Kayla.

But then he tilted up her chin and kissed her softly, and all she wanted to do was melt in his arms and let him bury her fear beneath a torrent of sensation.

"I'm making you some dinner," he said, as she greeted Sampson. "I hope you're hungry."

Angela had been so preoccupied that she hadn't bothered to eat. "I am hungry," she admitted and ignored the voice that was yelling *Tell him!* in the corner of her mind.

They had all night, didn't they? She had to wait for the right moment.

STEPHANIE STOOD at the pay phone, cursing the long wait as other addicts called a boyfriend, a girlfriend, family. They were limited to one call a day and Stephanie had already taken her turn, but she didn't care. She pushed in front of several people, brushing aside their complaints. She needed to use the phone again, and no one was stopping her.

Was Angela moving to Virginia City? Was *that* what was going on? Or was she taking Kayla to her father?

After she'd found out she was pregnant, her mother's reaction was the only reason Stephanie hadn't told Matt. She'd wanted to let him know about the baby, could hardly wait to break the news that he *had* to notice her now. That she had something no one else did, even his beloved Danielle. She'd never seen her mother as angry as she'd been the day she'd learned—thanks to Angela— exactly what Stephanie had done. Betty had promised right then that if Stephanie ever told Matt about Kayla—if she ever told *anyone* the name of Kayla's father—it would be the last straw. Betty would disown Stephanie, and she'd be out on her ass. For real. No family. No friends. No one to catch her when she fell.

Deep in her heart, Stephanie had known she needed her mother too much to sever that tie. And, in her more honest moments, she'd also known that even if Matt had accepted Kayla, he would never fully accept Stephanie. So she'd been forced to stick with her only form of support. She had to save herself one last chance, always. Betty was her ticket to a better life, when she'd finally had enough.

Once she'd grown older, however, she hadn't used that chance and she'd rarely thought of Matt. He hadn't been much of a partier in high school. She knew he wouldn't approve of her and didn't need his arrogant judgments.

But neither did she need Angela thinking she could take Betty's place now that Betty was dead. Angela had told Stephanie she had to clean up if she wanted to be part of her daughter's life. Yet Angela had no right to make such a stipulation. Stephanie had only signed those guardianship papers, giving Kayla to her mother, because she'd been desperate for a few bucks. Angela wasn't even related to Kayla. How could Betty have signed Kayla over to her? Angela was a parasite her mother had picked up long ago, and now the flea thought she owned the dog.

Memories of her friend pleading with her to take control of her life threatened to undermine Stephanie's resolve, as did an underlying knowledge that Kayla was probably better off without a mother like her, but Stephanie wouldn't allow it. As long as Angela had Kayla, Angela couldn't turn Stephanie away.

But Angela's return to Virginia City seemed to confirm Stephanie's worst fear. Was it over? Was Angela *really* giving up on her?

At last, Stephanie reached the front of the line. Behind her, she could hear two women complaining about how pushy she'd been. She knew they might report her. She'd leave the shelter if they did. This call meant that much to her.

She held the receiver, her hands shaking from withdrawal, but also from the emotions pounding through her. Her daughter was the one good thing that had ever happened to her. She couldn't let Angela turn Kayla over to Matt.

"Operator. How can I help you?"

Stephanie drew a bolstering breath. She had to talk to someone who might've seen Angela, someone who might know what was going on. But who?

It took four tries—and all the change she'd won in a poker game earlier—before the operator actually had the number Stephanie had requested. "I'll put you through," she said.

Then the phone rang twice and Sheila Gilbert picked up.

"I have a collect call from Stephanie Cunningham. Will you accept the charges?"

There was a slight pause, followed quickly by a surprised, "Sure, no problem."

MATT SAT AT ONE END of the couch facing Angela, who sat on the other. Sampson lay contently between them, stretched out at their feet. They'd had dinner and talked about his family, his job, her job, what it was like in Denver, how Virginia City had changed. He'd enjoyed the conversation, felt they'd connected in a way he hadn't connected with a woman in years. She hadn't touched him, but he still hoped the evening would end as he wanted it to. Imagining her as he'd seen her at his parents', her head thrown back in wild abandon as he kissed her neck, bare shoulders and breasts, made his heart race.

He ached to touch her again. Would he get the same powerful reaction?

He certainly didn't want to spook her again. That night at his parents', everything had happened way too fast. This time, he was determined to slow things down. Maybe he could even convince her to stay the night.

He liked the thought of that. But he felt it was important to talk about their other encounter. He had a feeling this relationship could be different from the casual flings he'd had with various women since Danielle, and that made him nervous. For the first time in ages, he wanted something he could lose. Especially because Angela didn't seem receptive to anything serious. And she lived two states away.

Obviously, there'd have to be some kind of compromise if they were going to build anything long-term out of their tremendous attraction.

"About the other night…" he began.

She lifted her eyes above the rim of her glass. She'd refused wine and was having cranberry juice. "What about it?" she asked as she set the glass aside, suddenly cautious.

"I'm confused," he admitted. "I can tell you're not interested in letting me touch you again, and yet…I thought you enjoyed it."

She cleared her throat. "I did."

Frowning, he studied her. "Then why—"

"It's not a matter of *want*," she said, still guarded.

"So…you're upset because it was too fast? More than you bargained for? What?"

"No." She tucked her hair behind one ear, giving him the impression she was stalling, thinking. "I—having you there, touching me, kissing me…it got the better of me, that's all. I knew I shouldn't let myself be swept away. But it'd been so long since I'd made love…and it'll probably be a long time before I do it again."

Matt felt as if she'd kicked him in the stomach. "You're saying it wasn't necessarily *me* you wanted. I just happened to come along and I could provide what had been missing from your life?"

"Matt, I'm dealing with a lot right now. I

can't worry about my own needs and desires. Like I said, that got the best of me, but now I've got to—"

"The other night you said my name as if I was the only man in the world," he interrupted. "You arched into me as if you'd abandon your soul to me, too, if you could."

Her jaw dropped as she gaped at him. "What do you want me to say?" she replied. "That I wish circumstances were different? That I wish we had a chance? Because I do. I want to make love with you right now. It's all I can do to keep from reliving those minutes, to keep from wanting you again! But—"

Matt's body had reacted instantly to her passionate words. He wanted the same thing. Here on the couch, on the table, anywhere. He couldn't remember ever feeling so desperate for another woman. "But?" he echoed.

"There's something I have to tell you."

The gravity in her voice made him uneasy. But she'd already insisted she wasn't married. Twice. So, as far as he could see, what she had to say couldn't be too bad. Nothing big enough to come between them, anyway. "What's that?" he asked.

She hugged herself as if she were almost too frightened to proceed. He was tempted to reach out and pull her to him, to comfort her, but he waited.

"Kayla isn't really my daughter," she said. "I—I was lying about that. She came to live with me fifteen months ago."

He blinked. That was surprising but certainly not devastating.

"She *feels* like my daughter. I *love* her like a daughter."

He would've felt relieved, except the tears filling Angela's eyes kept him a little off balance. "Of course you do," he said gently. "I understand."

"No, you don't." She wrung her hands as the tears spilled down her cheeks. "You see…there was no man who walked out on us. She—she's *Stephanie's* daughter."

He tried that on for size. *This* was supposed to be the big shocker? That Angela was raising Stephanie's daughter? He hoped so, because it didn't take longer than a split second to realize he could love Kayla regardless of what he felt for Stephanie. It actually made sense. Stephanie was much more likely to get herself in trouble than Angela, who'd been cautious even back in high school.

"It's okay," he said. "I'm cool with that."

She dashed a hand across her face. "I'm not finished."

Sliding closer, he took her hand. "Whatever you have to say, it's going to be fine."

She closed her eyes. "Kayla's grandmother was raising her. I—I took her to live with me when her grandmother died."

"Why didn't Stephanie step up?" he asked. "You said she was in Denver, in sales or something."

She opened her eyes and her hand gripped his like a lifeline. "Stephanie's a heroin addict, Matt. The only thing she sells is her body. She—she's not the person I once knew. I've finally come to the conclusion that it's not safe for Kayla to be around her."

"Wow." He reached out to smooth the hair from her forehead. "I'm sorry to hear that. Sorry for you and for Kayla. But it doesn't change what's between us."

Her forehead creased in a troubled expression. "Remember that party?" she asked.

"What party?"

"In high school."

That party. With Stephanie naked. Where

he'd had one of his first sexual encounters. *Sexual* encounters…

Fear struck and Matt dropped her hand. "*Yes?*"

Angela looked bereft, as if she'd reach out to him, but didn't. "Matt, I brought Kayla here because she belongs to you."

Matt rocked back and pressed both hands to his chest, hardly able to breathe. How had Kayla gone from being *Angela's* daughter to being *his* daughter in just a few seconds? His and Stephanie's, who was now a prostitute and a drug addict!

"It…it can't be true," he said softly because his voice wouldn't go any louder.

"It *is* true," she insisted. "Stephanie wanted to get pregnant. She thought she'd finally be able to have you if she did. But when Betty found out what she was up to, she yanked us both out of school and we moved. Betty didn't want it to ruin your life. She knew how unfair it was to you, your family, your girlfriend, everyone."

He shook his head, still unable to believe what he was hearing. He'd slept with Stephanie *once!* And she'd drugged him to get that far. Now Angela was telling him he had a twelve-year-old daughter?

What do you want for Christmas?... I'd like to find my dad....

God! A blinding rage suddenly took hold of him and he shot to his feet. "You knew and yet...you came here, all the while knowing...You let me—" He stopped. Too many thoughts and feelings were assaulting him. He wasn't sure what he was trying to say. He felt so...manipulated. Then and now.

"I'm sorry," she whispered.

He stalked to the window so he wouldn't have to look at her and stared out. It was snowing again, coming down so thick he couldn't see more than a foot in front of him. What was he supposed to think? *What was he supposed to do?*

"What do you want from me?" he asked after a long silence.

She didn't answer right away. When he finally turned, she was standing and had her purse clutched tightly in her hands. "Nothing," she said. "I—I just thought you should know."

"Does *she* know?" he asked.

Angela shook her head. "I decided it'd be smarter to tell you first. This way...nothing *has* to change. I have everything I need to take care of her. But I...I didn't want to steal anything from you. Or take anything from her if...if you felt differently. That's all."

That was all. She'd given him the most shocking news of his life and now she was leaving with a simple "Oops—never mind."

He tried to focus on the act of breathing. He kept seeing Stephanie that night, her triumphant smile as Danielle had wept— and he felt sick.

He'd gotten her pregnant. He'd fathered a child at sixteen. And now that child was twelve years old and didn't know who her own daddy was.

CHAPTER NINE

NOTHING HAS TO CHANGE. Those words seemed to echo in Matt's head long after Angela left. They were so ridiculous. If what Angela had told him was true, if Kayla really belonged to him, *everything* had changed. Regardless of the way Kayla had been conceived, he couldn't simply go on as if he didn't know he had a daughter.

He'd get tests, of course—for his own peace of mind. Stephanie was the one behind this, and he didn't trust her one bit. But he was fairly sure DNA would confirm what he'd just been told. Kayla was his. Stephanie had been so obsessed with him, he doubted she'd so much as looked at another boy that entire year. And when he pictured Kayla, he could see the family resemblance. It was a wonder he hadn't noticed it before. Or maybe not. Why would he? He'd never even entertained the thought. Not after one incident he could hardly remember. And not after such a long silence.

I want to find my daddy....

Still at the window, Matt shoved a hand through his hair. *I'm your daddy.* The reality of that was overwhelming. And yet he felt a strong sense of responsibility. He had to tell Kayla. He couldn't let a child of his go through life feeling lost and unloved.

But how did he explain what had happened? And where did they go from here?

He needed to call Angela, get her to come back so they could talk. Now that the initial shock was beginning to wear off, he could see that she was in a difficult situation, as well. She wasn't to blame for Stephanie's actions thirteen years ago. And yet she was standing in for the absent parents, taking care of a child who wasn't even hers.

His child.

He wasn't convinced he'd ever get used to the idea.

Reaching for the cordless phone, he dialed the hotel. No answer. He tried her cell.

"This is Angela Forrester. I'm out of town

until after the holidays, but if you'll leave your name and number, I'll return your call as soon as I can. If this is an emergency, please contact my assistant, Lisa Burton, at Pierpont Realty."

The beep sounded in Matt's ear. "This is an emergency, but your assistant can't help me. I need you. I'm sorry if I didn't react the way you'd hoped I would. I admit that I'm still...reeling. But I need to talk to you, to discuss this. Can I come over? Or if you find that too threatening, you can come here."

Frustrated, he punched the off button and was about to toss the phone across the counter when it rang.

"Thank God," he muttered and answered immediately, although caller ID said Unknown. He assumed Angela had her cell number blocked. But it wasn't Angela.

"I have a collect call from Stephanie Cunningham."

Matt stiffened. *Stephanie* was calling him? After thirteen years of silence? That scared the hell out of him. He hadn't even decided what he was going to do about Kayla and already Stephanie was back in his life!

"Will you accept the charges?" the operator asked.

He cursed silently to himself but agreed. Then Stephanie's voice came across the line.

"Matt, don't listen to her," she said in a rush. "It's a lie."

He expected to feel a wave of intense hatred, especially now that he knew the real consequences of what she'd done to him, but he didn't. A variety of other emotions surged through him instead—anger, pity and disgust. He'd never imagined Stephanie as part of his future. Had he just stepped into some alternate reality?

"*What's* a lie?" he asked, pacing in agitation. Sampson whined, obviously sensing something wrong, but Matt ignored him.

"You don't need to give Kayla any locket. She's not yours. She's from…someone else, a—a guy I met after I left Virginia City."

Matt wished he could believe her—so his life would return to normal. He almost asked her for Kayla's birthday so he could compare the dates. But he didn't need to. The hard edge of desperation in Stephanie's voice told him she was the one who was lying. And now that he'd heard the truth, there was no hiding from it. "What are you hoping to gain by telling me that?" he asked.

"I'm doing you a favor. You're off the hook. You're not the father. Tell Angela she has to come home now. She—she can't leave me here. She can't take my child away from me."

So he wasn't the only one frightened by recent developments. They were all scared, he realized. His involvement upset the delicate equilibrium. And yet Angela had risked it.

"Where are you?" he asked.

"None of your business," she said, but he could hear others talking in the background—"Get off the phone, bitch. I get to make my call, too"—and imagined her in jail or some sort of community shelter.

Briefly, the temptation to take Stephanie at her word, skip the paternity test and pretend he'd never met Kayla reasserted itself. He didn't need to be part of this mess, did he? It wasn't his fault. Angela would take care of Kayla. She'd be fine.

And yet...

He focused on the statue he'd brought home from the station, the one Kayla and Angela had given him for Christmas. It was a fireman rescuing a child. *Safe from imminent danger.*

With a mother like Stephanie, what child needed him more desperately than his own?

"I'm sorry, Stephanie," he said. "But there are going to be some changes."

"What changes?" she cried.

His eyes still on the statue, he drew a deep breath. "If Kayla's mine, I'll be taking care of her from now on."

ANGELA'S HEART BEGAN TO RACE the moment she heard Matt banging on her door. What now? She'd managed to avoid his calls, but she could hardly let him wake all the other hotel guests at one o'clock in the morning.

Dropping his quilt, which she'd been hugging around her since she'd finished packing Kayla's and her belongings, she hurried across the room and opened the door to find a rumpled-looking Matt.

"Let me in," he said, his voice terse, his eyes intense.

Angela didn't want to. She regretted telling him about Kayla and longed to go home, to pretend that what they'd said and done here in Virginia City had never happened. Tomorrow night was Christmas Eve, but she'd drive straight through. She couldn't wait.

"Matt—"

He peered over her head at the luggage. "It's too late to run," he said.

Someone across the hall peered out, wearing a disgruntled expression, and Angela quickly waved Matt inside.

"I'm not running. I'm—"

"Heading home." He glowered at the bags. "Two states away, which probably sounds like a pretty safe distance."

"I thought maybe we should...you know, take the next few weeks to consider the situation. You can call me in Denver when—"

"I've considered it," he interrupted.

The determination in his voice sent terror shooting through Angela. He had something to say already? She'd only left his place a couple of hours ago. "What have you decided?" she whispered.

He reached over to run his thumb along Kayla's name, which was embroidered on the backpack she'd brought for her beloved books. "I want her. She's mine. I'll take care of her from here on out."

Tears sprang to Angela's eyes. "Matt, wait. Please, I..." The lump in her throat choked off her words. She wasn't sure what to say, anyway. She knew Kayla wanted her father more than anything and that Matt would be good to her. She also knew he could offer her a loving extended family, the roots she craved and greater protection from the influence of her mother. The distance alone would be a plus, because Stephanie couldn't stop by every time she was down and out and wanted money for drugs.

Angela should let Kayla go, shouldn't she? But the thought of driving home without her, of packing up all her belongings and shipping them off, broke Angela's heart. She'd hoped to convince Matt that they could share Kayla, despite the thousand miles that separated them, but the words wouldn't come. It wasn't a realistic idea, anyway. One of them would have to play a very minor role in Kayla's life. And she knew which one that should be.

She breathed deeply, trying to absorb the pain, and felt his hand at her elbow.

"You okay?" he murmured.

Fresh tears fell as she looked up at him. "No," she said. Then his arms went around her, as his quilt had a few minutes earlier, and his mouth touched hers in a kiss that spoke of warmth and comfort—but quickly changed to driving passion and escalating need.

MATT WOKE UP IN Angela's bed. He could smell the clean scent of her hair, feel the softness of her bare skin as she continued to sleep with her body curled into his side, and knew that he'd gained more than a daughter last night. He wanted Angela, too. He wasn't sure how they were going to work out the logistics—where they'd live and who would change jobs—but he was hoping she'd marry him so they could become a family.

He smiled wryly at the thought of that. A *family?* A week ago, he hadn't even had a girlfriend.

He adjusted the quilt they'd used to cover themselves, the quilt he'd given Angela for Christmas, and his smile widened. Just when he'd begun to think it would never happen…

"You're awake?" Angela murmured.

He'd been cautious with his movements so he wouldn't disturb her, but now he slid his hand up over the curve of her hip to her breast, as he'd wanted to do ever since he'd opened his eyes.

"Aren't you tired?" she asked, covering a yawn. "We were up all night."

"I feel good. What about you?"

She gave him a sexy smile. "Fishing for compliments?"

He chuckled. "You kidding? Your screams were enough. I'm surprised our neighbors didn't complain to the management."

"I didn't scream that loud!" She tried to sit up in mock outrage, but he pressed her back, too busy enjoying what his fingers had found.

"Okay, but you groaned a lot," he said. "I loved it. And the way you looked at me right before you—"

She tried to brush his hand away. "Do we have to go over the details?"

"Why are you embarrassed?" He laughed as he moved her beneath him. "I told you I loved it. And the marks on my back will

_____rowed her eyes. "I didn't leave _____our back!"

_____"There's always this

morning." He kissed the indentation beneath her ear. "And the morning after." He kissed the pulse at her neck. "And the morning after that." He let his mouth drift lower, enjoying the fact that he could so easily make her quiver.

"No, I'm going home today...remember?" She gave a little gasp on that last word because he'd hit his real target.

"It's the holidays," he said, blowing cool air on the breast he'd just suckled.

She was getting lost in his lovemaking. He could tell. But she fought it. "So?"

"So you're spending Christmas with me."

"Trying to get another gift out of me?" she teased.

Leaving her breast, he kissed a trail down to her navel. "No, something better."

"What's that?" she asked, but he knew she was having a difficult time concentrating. He was making sure of it.

"A promise."

"What...kind...of promise?"

He didn't answer. He was too busy.

"Matt!" Her hands clenched in his hair.

He wasn't sure if she'd said his name by way of question or encouragement. But she seemed pretty interested in holding him right where he was, so he guessed she'd been en-couraging him—and waited until just the right moment to answer. When her eyes closed, and her muscles tensed, she said his name again, only this time with power and more than a little urgency, and when the moment passed, he told her what he really wanted.

"Marry me."

ANGELA SAT IN THE living room of Matt's parents' home, enjoying Christmas morning. Outside, sunlight glistened on the snow and the world around them appeared crisp and bright, silent and peaceful. Inside, Christ-mas music played softly in the background as Sherry handed out mugs of hot chocolate and Kayla helped Matt's two younger cousins sort the Christmas presents, which they planned to open in a few minutes. Angela had brought some gifts for Kayla, so Kayla had a small pile of her own, but Matt had something far better waiting for her. Today was the day she'd get exactly what she wanted for Christmas: She'd learn the identity of her father.

"You nervous?" Matt murmured. He'd

been sitting next to Angela since she and Kayla had arrived a few minutes earlier.

Angela nodded. "Dying. You?"

"Yeah."

He seemed excited. He also seemed intent on making them a family. Angela had asked him not to mention the possibility to Kayla. She needed more time to think. She had a home and a career in Colorado. Pulling up stakes and moving back to Virginia City was a big decision. Especially so soon. And then there was Stephanie...

When Matt had told Angela about his conversation with Kayla's mother, Angela had made some calls, trying to locate her. It was so difficult to give up hope. She'd thought maybe Stephanie was ready to get clean at last. But when she'd finally made contact with the shelter where Stephanie had been staying, she'd been told that a man named Jaydog had picked her up late last night.

That was where the trail had gone cold. Stephanie was probably right back on the streets, doing anything she could to feed her addiction. Angela had been through the cycle enough times to know that—and yet she felt so guilty for loving Matt, for wanting to be with him. Could she really move back to Virginia City with Stephanie's daughter and agree to marry the boy Stephanie had wanted so desperately?

She didn't think so.

"He's asked her to marry him," Angela heard Sherry whisper to Ray, Ray's wife and Claudia, her sister, in the kitchen. "Can you believe it? He's in love!"

Angela glanced worriedly at Kayla, afraid she might overhear. But Kayla didn't even look up. She was too busy burrowing under the tree.

"What did she say?" came Ray's murmured response.

"She's thinking about it." Sherry lowered her voice, but Angela could still make out the words. "So be really nice to her."

Evidently, Matt had heard his mother, too, because he squeezed Angela's hand and Angela couldn't help laughing softly to herself.

"So where would they live?" Claudia asked.

"I'm praying it'll be here. What good is getting my first granddaughter if I never get to see her?"

Matt's mother had a point. If they got

married, they'd live in Virginia City. Angela knew that already. But even if they didn't marry, Kayla would stay with Matt. Angela felt certain she'd be happier here than she'd been in Denver. The only decision left was whether or not Angela could allow herself to be part of the idyllic picture. Could she say yes? After everything Betty had done for her, did she have that right?

"We're ready!" Kayla shouted.

Sherry ushered in the group from the kitchen, while Claudia's children rounded up their dad and Matt's father, who'd been checking out the new computer in the other room.

Matt let go of Angela's hand and leaned his elbows on his knees, watching Kayla as she sat next to her presents.

"Do we take turns like before? Or do we all open at once?" she asked.

When Matt stood, Angela knew he couldn't wait any longer. "Before we get too carried away with all the gifts, I have something to say."

Sherry grabbed her husband's arm excitedly, Ray grinned at his wife and Claudia motioned for complete silence. Obviously, except for the children, they all thought they knew what he was about to announce. But this would be a surprise.

Angela clasped her hands tightly in her lap.

"I have a special gift for Kayla. One I'd like her to open now," Matt said.

Kayla sat up straighter. "But you already gave me a gift, Matt." Her hand went to her throat in search of her locket but, finding it missing, she turned worried eyes to Angela. "My locket! It's gone!"

"You haven't lost it," Angela said. "I took it last night. Matt's giving it to you again." She cleared her throat to help steady her voice. "Only this time it has your father's picture in it."

Silence as thick as the snowdrifts piled outside descended on the room as everyone stared at Kayla, who was still gazing in shock at Angela. "That can't be true," she said.

"It's true," Angela said.

Matt crossed the room and pulled the plush blue box from his pocket.

"Are you sure I should open it here?" she asked him.

He knelt down beside her so everyone could see. "It's okay," he murmured. "Go ahead."

Kayla's trepidation showed in the stiff set of her shoulders. With a final glance at the people watching, she slowly, carefully withdrew the locket.

Angela's pulse raced as Kayla opened the tiny clasp. Then the girl's jaw dropped and her gaze flew to Matt, who was watching her with so much hope that everyone in the room could feel the poignant emotions inside him.

"*You're* my dad? I mean, my *real* dad?"

Tears glistened in Matt's eyes. He kept blinking, obviously struggling to hold them back, but he nodded. "I just found out myself the day before yesterday. I'm glad I know," he said and gathered her in his arms.

Angela didn't realize she had tears rolling down her own cheeks until they began to drip off her chin. She wiped them as Kayla squeezed Matt tightly.

"Merry Christmas, Kayla," he said. Then he released her and turned her to face all the others in the room. "And these people— they're your family, too."

Sherry had nearly fainted at "You're my dad?" Now she leaned heavily on her husband and waved a hand in front of her, as if she couldn't get enough air. "Does that mean you're going to marry him?" she asked Angela hopefully.

She still believed what she'd originally been told—that Angela was Kayla's real mother. They could explain the details later, Angela decided. She had enough going on right now. Everyone's attention had shifted to her, even Kayla's.

"Marry him?" Kayla murmured.

"That—that's one option," Angela admitted. "We've been...talking about it."

"And what are the other options?" Kayla asked.

Everyone's eyes cut back and forth between them. Angela hoped no one could tell how badly she was shaking. "You could live here with...with Matt."

Some of the excitement fled Kayla's face. "Without you?"

"I don't know yet, Kayla. I have a house in Denver—"

"We're selling the house, remember?"

"And a job."

"Can't you work here?"

"You wouldn't have to. I can support you," Matt said.

His mother moved closer to him. "He'd make a good husband."

"And you've seen the calendar," his aunt added. "You know what kind of fires he can put out."

Angela didn't have a chance to answer any of them. Kayla's eyebrows were drawing together in hurt and anger. "You said I'd always be a central part of your life, and no one would ever change that. Now you're giving me away?"

"I'm not giving you away," Angela said. "I—I'm letting you live where I think you'll be happiest."

"I can't be happy without you!"

Angela turned to Matt, expecting him to help her defer answering. But he didn't. "I can't be happy without you, either," he said softly, honestly.

"Do you love him?" Sherry asked.

Angela didn't want to admit the truth. She knew what would happen. But Matt was watching her so intently, she couldn't lie. "I do."

"So say *yes*... Marry him...It's Christmas," everyone said, pressing closer.

Angela let her uncertainty show in her expression. "What about Stephanie?" she asked, seeking Matt. "Kayla's *her* daughter. You're the man *she* wanted."

This threw the others, but not Matt. "We'll do what we can for her," he promised. "When she's ready."

Kayla's arms slipped around Angela's waist. "Leaving us won't help her!" she said, hugging her tightly. And it was those words that finally made sense to Angela. Denying herself the joy of being with Matt and Kayla wouldn't help anyone.

The tears started to come again, but Angela brushed them away. "Yes."

"You'll do it?" Kayla cried. "You'll marry him?"

Angela smiled through her tears. "I will."

Matt's arms went around both of them, and he kissed Angela's temple. "I'll make sure you never regret it," he whispered.

The rest of the group hugged and congratulated her one by one, and Angela smiled as she realized that Kayla's new family had just become her own.

Maybe this Christmas wasn't like the ones she used to know. But she knew there'd never be a better one. Except for next year. And the years after that...

Dear Reader,

I've always had a fondness for the story of Scrooge and his journey to become a better person. When Brenda Novak, Anna Adams and I first started brainstorming ideas for this project, I found myself intrigued by the idea of Scrooge (Simon Castle in my story) falling in love with the Ghost of Christmas Present (Emma Roberts). Okay, so Emma isn't a ghost and Simon doesn't wear a full-length nightshirt, but the idea that someone can make a difference in your perspective on life is fascinating. I hope you enjoy my lighthearted take on this classic tale.

I love to hear from readers, either through my Web site, www.melindacurtis.com, or regular mail at P.O. Box 150, Denair, CA 95316. Bah, humbug...er...happy holidays!

Melinda Curtis

THE NIGHT BEFORE CHRISTMAS
Melinda Curtis

As always, to my family, especially my kids, who constantly remind me what's important in life. And for Mom, whose patience and enduring love gave me the strength to reach for the stars.

CHAPTER ONE

SIMON CASTLE NEEDED an exterminator, preferably one with a law degree.

Stepping out of the dark casino into the late afternoon sunlight, he frowned as he scanned the empty circular drive in front of his hotel. Not only was his car missing, but the rat—tall, gray and menacing—was still holed up in the west parking lot, where it had been taunting him since last night.

"It's still there, sir," Carrie, his latest assistant, observed. "Do you want me to call someone?"

"No." Tension rat-a-tat-tatted at Simon's temples.

The fifteen-foot inflatable rat—complete with pointed, retractable claws—was the labor union's latest attempt to bully him. Simon could deflate the vermin or have the truck it sat in towed, but that would only bring bad press. Exactly what the union wanted. If the union wanted to solve the dispute, the reps could come back to the bargaining table. Simon didn't respond to intimidation.

He clenched his fingers, fighting the urge to charge across the parking lot and take matters into his own hands. Instead, Simon issued an order to Carrie. "Put a garland around its neck. Maybe the guests will think it's a promotion for *The Nutcracker.* Now, where's my car?"

He couldn't wait until the holiday season was over.

Carrie hit the speed dial on her cell phone, turned away and spoke discreetly to Simon's secretary, Marlene, through the headset clipped over her ear. A moment later, clutching her clipboard to her chest, Carrie stumbled as she turned back in her four-inch heels. "Uh, apparently, there was a mix-up, sir. Frank thought we were done for the holiday weekend."

Simon waved off the explanation. "Fine. Have someone else bring the car around." Icy wind whipped at him and he shrugged deeper into his overcoat. He glanced at his watch, ignoring the discreet holiday music and oversize Christmas decorations looming above him. "I have to be in Vegas by morning."

On the twelfth day of Christmas my true love gave to me...

As if some guy was sappy enough to send his woman twelve lords-a-leaping, or a woman would be satisfied with the display. Women wanted money and attention. They were a distraction Simon couldn't afford.

Carrie pressed the speaker to her ear as she paused, obviously listening to Marlene. Then her mouth popped open. Carrie quickly closed it, cleared her throat and said, "Um, apparently Frank took the car."

"Fine. Give him a call and get it back." Simon was already calculating what business he could conduct while he waited for Frank to make the forty-five-minute drive from Simon's home above the Northgate Golf Club to the Castle Hotel. He headed toward the casino where the rat could no longer taunt him.

"Uh, sir?" Carrie trotted up next to him.

"Spit it out, Carrie," Simon snapped.

"Frank took the car to Los Angeles for the holiday weekend."

His temple pounded as he spun to face her. "What? Who gave him permission to do that?" Whoever it was would be fired. And Frank along with him.

"Apparently—"

Simon was starting to hate that word.

"—*you* signed the paperwork, sir. It's dated three months ago." Carrie paused, listening to Marlene read something. "Apparently—"

"Oh, for the love of—" Simon bit back the rest of his curse. Carrie was his fourth assistant in as many months. Turnover was getting damn annoying because the talent pool was sadly lacking in Reno.

"His mother is having surgery. He'll be taking time off until the new year."

"With my car?" Simon snatched Carrie's earpiece. "Marlene, get me on the next plane to Vegas and fill out Frank's termination paperwork." Simon had never been invited to a meeting of the heads of all the best Nevada casinos before, so he wasn't going to miss this one tomorrow morning. He had to prove he wasn't small potatoes to the likes of casino magnates Steven Wynn and George Maloof.

Why did everything have to fall apart today?

"No can do, boss. Everything's booked," Marlene said.

The opportunity to make something of himself was slipping through Simon's fingers as surely as that annoying chorus of "The Twelve Days of Christmas" would haunt him until Judgment Day.

His father's voice boomed ominously in his head. "You can either care for people or make something of yourself, boy. And, in the end, everyone will let you down anyway, so you may as well make something of yourself."

The rat rocked back and forth in the wind as if laughing at Simon. His father would have given it the finger. Simon clenched his fists.

"The rental car agencies are all sold out." Marlene's fingers clacked over the keyboard. "I might be able to get you on a bus with one of those senior tours, sir. I'll see if they have a cancellation."

Simon's back tensed. Had it really come to this? He and sixty shuffling old folks on a bus?

More clacking. "Those are all booked, too. What do you want me to do?"

A shiny, black Lincoln Town Car with a worn wreath strapped to the front grill pulled around the bend of the hotel's driveway.

"I'll get to Vegas on my own." Simon handed the earpiece back to Carrie, intent upon the approaching vehicle.

"HERE YOU GO, LADIES. The Castle Hotel," Emma Roberts announced as she turned off "The Twelve Days of Christmas" and put the Town Car in park. "It's the best place in town for single men over sixty."

The two seventy-year-old women giggled like schoolgirls when they spotted a pair of gray-haired men who had stepped outside to light cigars. Emma loved driving people around during the holidays, sharing their joy and excitement. Her business had been booming since Thanksgiving and all her fares had been brimming with seasonal cheer. Not a Scrooge in sight.

Grinning, Emma hustled around to open the car door for her two passengers, and then unloaded their luggage, transferring care of the two suitcases and cosmetic cases to the bellboy. She graciously accepted her payment and closed the trunk.

Christmas may now begin.

Not. A suit with his ear glued to a cell phone was sitting in her backseat. He hadn't even closed the door after he'd gotten in.

Emma walked around to his side. "I'm sorry, sir, but I'm done for the day." It was Christmas Eve and she had to get to Virginia City to be with her family.

The suit ignored her.

No one but casino management—the lowest of the low—wore a *suit* in Reno. Emma should know. She had contracts with many of the hotels in Reno. Management tended to be cold, snooty and poor tippers.

A blonde, also in a suit, rushed forward on wobbly stiletto heels. "Excuse me." She pulled Emma away from the car by her arm. "Mr. Castle requires a ride to Las Vegas."

Emma frowned up at the hotel marquee. Castle Hotels was one of Nevada's newer and smaller casino chains. She'd never seen Mr. Castle. And she had no desire to meet him today.

"Don't you mean Mr. Castle needs a ride to the airport? So he can *fly* to Las Vegas?" Emma regained possession of her arm and stepped toward the car, intent on getting rid of the businessman. "I'll drop him on my way home."

"No." Blondie cut off her retreat. "I'll double whatever you normally charge if you *drive* Mr. Castle to Las Vegas." In the fifty-degree weather, even without a warm coat, Blondie's mascara was smudged. She was sweating, not so tough after all.

Emma resisted smiling. "Why don't you drive him? It's Christmas Eve and—"

"I have a little boy," the other woman whispered, clearly desperate. "One thousand dollars. Cash."

Whatever protest Emma had been about to make died on her lips, as she visualized a heartbroken child without his mother on Christmas. Besides, one thousand dollars would keep the Town Car juiced for quite some time. "The price of gas has been eating me alive," Emma mumbled.

"I don't care what it costs. I need to be in Vegas tonight." Mr. Castle leaned forward, not far enough that Emma could see more than his chin, what with the phone glued to his ear and the body of the car blocking the rest of her view. She couldn't see his face, couldn't judge if he was a pretty boy or someone to be reckoned with. But his voice...

His tone demanded she obey without regard for holidays or family plans.

Emma blinked.

Here was a man sadly lacking in the spirit

of the Christmas. If she was her father's daughter, she'd turn down the cash and drive Mr. Castle to Las Vegas for nothing more than gas money, showing him the true holiday spirit. Christopher Roberts had been generous to a fault, at the expense of his checking account.

"There are no more flights available and Mr. Castle has to be in Las Vegas for a breakfast meeting."

"I'm sorry. I promised my mother I'd spend Christmas Eve with her in Virginia City."

Blondie's eyes widened. "Virginia City is on the way."

"It's about an hour out of his way not counting any stops I need to make." Emma had some sympathy for the woman, but she'd heard nothing that would persuade her to change her plans.

"Two thousand." Blondie leaned around Emma to sneak a peek at her boss. *Two thousand dollars.*

"Two grand? Just to drive him to Las Vegas?" The lure of the money was strong, stronger than it should have been. She wasn't living up to her father's standards. But if Emma took the job, she'd have more than twenty bucks to donate to the Santa Express charity this year.

And how much will you keep for yourself? It was a mind-numbing question considering Emma lived hand-to-mouth.

Capitalizing on Emma's hesitation, Castle's assistant leaned into the car and told her boss they'd be stopping along the way.

Something mechanical hummed on the pavement behind Emma. A thin woman with white hair haloed by a phone headset, the cord dangling at her waist, guided her wheelchair to a stop in front of Emma and thrust a wad of bills at her. "Here. I'm Marlene, Mr. Castle's secretary. I think twenty-*five* hundred dollars is fair."

Emma found herself holding the thick wad of folded Benjamins while Blondie sealed Mr. Castle in the car.

"Do whatever he asks," Blondie said. "There's a bonus in it for you if he's happy when he gets there. Mr. Castle can be somewhat exacting in his standards."

"Give me your card, dear, so I can make sure you're compensated for any incidents." The woman in the wheelchair held out her hand for Emma's business card, which doubled as a receipt. "Try not to mention too much about the holiday. It annoys him."

"It's *Christmas Eve*." This was a bad idea. She should just toss those twenty-five hundred-dollar bills back....

She was momentarily mesmerized by all that green in her hand. And there was Mr. Castle, who couldn't be as heartless as he sounded if he employed the grandmotherly woman in the wheelchair. Emma could make Christmas wonderful for a lot of families with that money.

"He's waiting." Blondie's voice sounded a bit strangled.

"He doesn't like to wait," added the older woman, glancing anxiously at the car as she wheeled her chair back.

Emma stuffed the cash in her pocket and got in the car. She would drive Mr. Castle to Las Vegas, stop to check in with her family and donate her profits to the Santa Express.

Now if only she didn't have to tell her mother she wouldn't be home for Christmas.

CHAPTER TWO

"TO LAS VEGAS." On that cheery note, the driver slid into her seat. Her white tuxedo shirt and black pants were acceptable, the red bow tie with green wreaths an unwelcome holiday reminder. "Your assistant did tell you that we're making a stop this evening?"

Damn it, he'd like to get some sleep tonight. Simon didn't have time for delays. He stared at the back of her head as he formulated a scathing reply. Stared at the driver's red-red hair held up in a bun against the creamy skin at her nape. "And if I said she didn't tell me?" he drawled. That came out completely, mischievously, inappropriately wrong.

"We're still stopping in Virginia City," she said firmly. "I hadn't counted on taking another fare today and my family is expecting me."

Simon frowned. Carrie had mentioned that the driver had to make a detour, but Simon had assumed she meant to get gas or to eat or something. Then again, he'd been meaning to check out the possibilities for a Castle property on the outskirts of Virginia City. The small town was an out-of-the-way tourist attraction with only a few small hotels.

"Mr. Castle?" With the sun dropping behind the Sierras, Simon could see the chauffeur's eyes dart to the mirror and back to the driveway. Why hadn't she started the car? "If that's a problem, I can drop you somewhere else." She sounded hopeful.

"It's inconvenient, but it'll do."

"What's with the rat?" she asked, finally starting the engine.

Refusing to look, Simon played dumb. "What rat?"

"Parked in a handicapped space—big, inflatable? Looks like he's on crack?"

"Oh, that." Simon tapped out an urgent e-mail on his BlackBerry reminding Carrie to choke the rat in festive garland.

"You're not presenting a topless version of *The Nutcracker* in your lounge, are you?"

Did the woman ever shut up? "A driver and a comedienne. It must be Christmas."

"Touchy about your rat infestation, I see." She pulled into heavy traffic. "Is that a symbol for something? Your logo perhaps?"

"It's not my logo." Simon leaned forward, making sure she heard every word clearly. "That's a union calling card. They think I should pay my maids more for working less. And I'm not happy to see that parasite in my parking lot, but I've got a reputation to protect, so I can't just exterminate it." Maybe now that he'd cut to the chase, she'd shut up.

"Are you paying the maids well?"

Through gritted teeth, Simon said. "I'm paying them the same as every other hotel."

"So the union is picking on you for no reason. That sucks."

"Yeah." She didn't need to know about the gripes of the chefs and cashiers.

With a nod, the woman turned up her stereo and began humming along to the music. Simon returned a call from his Reno hotel manager and quickly became irritated when Richard babbled nonstop about his problems on the property. So much for Richard living up to the claim on his résumé of being a problem solver. Why hadn't he said anything to Simon when he was in the office?

On the eleventh day of Christmas, my true love gave to me...

Eleven pipers piping. As if there was anything to be piping up about at this time of year. With a flick of a finger, Simon put Richard on hold. "Turn that down."

"What?" She lowered the sound.

"The music. Turn it down. I need to get work done."

The slant of her eyes in the mirror was disapproving. "Just trying to spread a little cheer. It is Christmas, after all."

"Well, save it for someone else." Someone who had happy memories of Christmas. Someone who looked forward to the holiday.

Simon drew a deep breath and listened as his manager droned on about employees who wanted time off and maids who wouldn't risk the wrath of the rat to come to work. "Richard, it's this simple. The employees either come in on Christmas or they don't come in ever again."

Was it his imagination, or did the driver tilt her head and frown at him in the mirror?

"But you aren't even offering a bonus," Richard continued nervously. "I have five hundred rooms booked and only two maids tomorrow. No one will come in just for time and a half. Not on Christmas."

"Bring in Carrie and the rest of the office staff. Between you and the two maids, you ought to be able to handle it." Simon hung up in disgust. When he went to Carson City next week, he was getting rid of Richard. Simon had come a long way without anyone guiding his every step. He wasn't the hand-holding type. His dad had seen to that.

His cell phone rang again—a Las Vegas area code.

"Mr. Castle, this is Erik Wiseman, assistant to Mr. Maloof. I'm calling to confirm your attendance tomorrow morning." Maloof's assistant spoke with just the right amount of disdain required when speaking to a nobody.

As if he could be seen through the telephone connection, Simon sat up straighter. "I—I—I'll be there." Damn. He couldn't believe he'd stuttered. He must have come across like an idiot.

"Doors close at six-fifteen sharp. Mr. Maloof has private plans later in the morning, as do several other attendees, but this is the only day of the year everyone's in town. Are you sure you won't have a family conflict?"

As if Simon would consider turning the offer down if he did. This was some kind of test that Simon was determined to pass. He shook his head, then realized Maloof's assistant couldn't see him. "No."

"Do you have any questions, Mr. Castle?"

"No. I'm en route." Nothing could stop Simon from getting there on time. "See you tomorrow."

Maloof's assistant broke the connection without so much as a *Merry Christmas*. He was Simon's kind of guy. Why couldn't more people be like that?

His driver pulled onto the freeway, the chorus of the dreaded Christmas song barely audible above the road noise.

"Could you turn that off?"

Her fingers didn't move from the steering wheel. "Are you going to be cranky all the way to Vegas?" She smiled into the rearview mirror.

Smiled. As if he were a child and she was trying to tease him into a better mood, as if they had a relationship other than client and service provider. Simon was momentarily speechless. No one who worked for him talked back. Certainly no one smiled at him like that.

"I thought *I* was paying *you*," Simon said finally, putting enough ice in his tone to frost her windshield.

"I can still drop you off at the airport, where you can stand in line for a flight." There was that optimistic note in her voice again, as if she wanted to get rid of him.

"I'd want my money back," he retorted, calling her bluff. "All of it." Simon wouldn't pay her to be stranded at the airport.

"Okay." She twisted in her seat and tossed the cash back to him.

Bills fluttered to the baseboards.

"What do you think you're doing?" He gathered up the notes. His father would have had a heart attack if he saw someone toss money around like that, as if it didn't matter.

"I'm planning on having a *merry* Christmas."

They were back to the ho-ho-ho crap. "We had a deal."

She merged into the exit lane for the airport. "Mr. Castle, I'm not your employee. I don't need your money."

"Everybody needs money."

She shook her head. "I'd rather spend Christmas with people who care about me than make a buck. Don't you have someone you'd like to spend the holiday with? Mother? Wife? Kids?"

The air in the car was suddenly stifling. Clutching the bills, Simon powered down his window a few inches, sucking in the cold mountain air. "I don't have any... It's none of your damn business."

"I'm sorry," she said in a voice that sounded amazingly sincere. "Do you prefer a particular terminal?" They'd exited the freeway.

"I need to get to Las Vegas!" He sounded about as adult as a five-year-old. Simon powered the window back up and loosened his tie. His driver really was going to drop him at the airport. Who did she think she was?

"I'd like to help you, but at the rate we're going, I'd probably leave you on the side of the road come Tonopah."

They sailed through every intersection as if the driver had some special ability to turn lights green. Simon was running out of time. There'd be nothing at the airport but lines and run-down local cabs. He couldn't call Maloof's assistant and back out now.

"Are you one of those cheer-mongers?" Simon accused. His driver didn't answer. "You know, the type who live for the holidays—bake the cookies, trim the tree, send out Christmas cards?"

"Did I hear you say *bah, humbug?*" she countered, but she was grinning.

Hell, she was probably ecstatic that she was about to dump him.

The airport, jammed with cars, loomed in front of them. Think. Think. Everybody had a price. He'd wager…double or nothing. "Five thousand dollars!"

"Excuse me?" She spared him a surprised glance in the rearview mirror.

"Five thousand dollars," he repeated at a more civilized volume. "Cash." He'd be offering to buy her car next so he could drive himself.

"That must be some meeting."

"The most important of my career." With the support of the major Las Vegas properties, Simon could take Castle Hotels almost anywhere.

"Wow." His driver had room to get out of the turn lane, but she wasn't budging.

"So, what do you say?"

The light changed green. Cars ahead began to inch forward.

"Are you really good for the money?" She eyed him suspiciously, turning this time.

"Do I look like I'm not?" He had to admire her negotiation skills. He was sweating and he had no idea if she'd accept his proposal or not. It was all he could do to not offer a higher amount.

"Oh, boy." She shook her head and gave a little laugh. "All right, Mr. Castle, I'll drive you to Las Vegas. But you'll have to put up with my holiday cheer."

Simon's lip twitched. "Just drive."

CHAPTER THREE

"DO YOU GET RECEPTION on that gadget everywhere?"

Mr. Castle peered down at his cell phone, which seemed to have more options than a fully loaded Town Car. Her threat to drop him off at the airport had captured his attention for all of five minutes. The man's constant clacking on his handheld device grated on her nerves, as did his desire for silence. She couldn't imagine spending Christmas with him. Didn't he do anything except work?

Emma went back to humming "Let It Snow" loud enough for her passenger to hear.

If he didn't treat her like a nobody, he might have been a welcome passenger. With his dark good looks—not a hair out of place—Mr. Castle could give Christian Bale a run for sexiest man alive. She glanced at him in the rearview mirror. He was all angles and shadows, as interesting to look at as a statue, but about as cold and heavy.

He finished what he was doing and looked up. "Too many people take time off at the holidays. I'm trying to catch them before they go. That's why I want *quiet*."

It was a real joy-sapping quiet, too. Mr. Castle was in desperate need of some holiday spirit. She had more than enough to share. "When I'm driving, I like noise. Sometimes I sing, too."

"With passengers in the car?"

"As long as you love me so—let it snow, let it snow, let it snow!" Someday, someone would love her that much. She didn't want gifts, just passion and mutual respect. Someday...

"What did I do to deserve this?" her passenger muttered.

"You asked for a ride on Christmas Eve." She could see him shaking his head in the mirror, could imagine his frown. What would he look like when he smiled? Warm and welcoming?

Startled, Emma concentrated on driving. Lusting after clients was not a good thing.

"You're not going to squander the

money I'm paying you on Christmas presents someone won't even remember come Easter, are you?"

"The holiday is about more than presents. You'd have to be blind not to see that." Mr. Castle knew nothing of Christmas.

"Christmas has lost any meaning it may have once had." Without waiting for Emma to respond, he leaned forward, his breath warm on her neck. "Do you want to know why I find Christmas superfluous? Because most people wonder if they've bought enough for their kids so they don't feel guilty Christmas morning. You think I'm blind?" He slapped a hand on the seat back, making her jump. "Well, those families with two-point-five kids are haunted by the ghost of Christmas returns, the ghost of leftover spirit lingering in credit-card debt and the haunting specter of bankruptcy."

"Not everyone's like that." But her protest lacked weight as they drove past a packed shopping mall. Her father would be so disappointed in her. Why had she ever agreed to take Mr. Castle anywhere?

"You haven't been in a casino lately, have you?" He sank back into his seat, taking his warmth with him.

"So now Christmas is a crime?" Emma shook her head ruefully. She couldn't hope to convince this man that beneath all the trimmings, Christmas was a time for kindness and charity.

They drove in silence for several miles while Emma wrestled with her mood, which right about now was far from charitable. She itched to shake Mr. Castle until his teeth rattled.

Her passenger sighed and shifted in the backseat, settled, then shifted again. She heard coins jingling. "What's Virginia City like?"

That sounded friendly. Friendly was a step up from the harbinger of bah-humbug he'd been fifteen minutes earlier. A glance revealed he was staring out the window.

"It's a small town where people take care of each other." Emma loved it there.

"I hear it has a lot of charm. I bet they have a decent number of tourists."

"We get our share." Emma sounded more defensive than she would have liked, but there was something in his voice that struck her as too casual. "The shops are always filled with people."

"I'm more interested in the businesses. Hotels? Restaurants?"

And then she caught on. He was looking for more ways to pad his bank account. The only surprise was that he hadn't asked about casinos. "There are a few bed-and-break-fasts, a couple of small motels, and a handful of restaurants."

"Who's the biggest employer?" Again the casual tone, as if they were talking about the weather, not his potential investment prospects.

"I couldn't say." She wasn't going to help him commercialize her hometown. "Why do you ask?"

"You never know what opportunities a town may afford unless you ask," he replied, unfazed. "How much longer until Virginia City?"

"Hungry?" She gritted her teeth. He was probably going to stake out Virginia City like a con man, looking to milk the quaint town for all it was worth.

"As a matter of fact, yes. Are we there yet?"

"Almost, but you'll have to put yourself in my hands for dinner. Nothing will be open on Christmas Eve." The food wouldn't be anything like what Mr. Castle was used to. She hoped he was polite enough not to complain.

"Put myself in your hands," he repeated so softly she barely made out the words.

But only an idiot would miss the sexy inflection in his tone, respond to the innuendo. Warmth flared deep and low inside her.

Clearly, Mr. Castle and his money had been sent to test her. Emma wished she could send him on a few Santa Express deliveries. Then he'd understand. But they didn't have time for that this year. Not if she wanted to get him to Las Vegas in time for his 6:00 a.m. meeting.

"IS SOMEONE HAVING A PARTY?" Simon asked as his driver parked her car at the end of the block. The neighborhood was old. Cars jammed every space between driveways for blocks in each direction.

"It's the Santa Express." She removed her bow tie and began tugging at her bun. "Every year a bunch of us get together with donations of food, clothing and toys. We deliver them to the area's needy on Christmas Eve."

He'd been right. She was a do-gooder. Simon hit a button to illuminate his Black-Berry screen. There were no replies from any of his e-mails and he hadn't received a call in thirty minutes. The holiday slacking had begun. "How long will you be?"

His driver shook out her red hair, waves tumbling across the white shirt. The glow from a streetlight illuminated her face in the rearview mirror as she looked directly at him. Simon couldn't help but stare back. Her eyes were as green as a Christmas tree. Why hadn't he noticed that before?

"Mr. Castle, I don't think you understand. I told you that all the restaurants are closed. If you want dinner, come with me."

He *wanted* to scribble ideas for transforming Virginia City into a bigger tourist destination. The main drag had that small-town, snow-blanketed, Victorian charm. He smelled raw opportunity. "I don't want to impose."

"Suit yourself. But the next food is about a hundred miles from here…if the drive-through in Babbitt is open."

Fast food? He paused. "This town needs a twenty-four-hour buffet." And a five-star restaurant.

"The town is fine the way it is." She shuffled papers in the front seat. "You might want to leave your suit jacket in the car. The tie, too."

Simon groaned. He was going to eat with *those kind* of people—those who scraped by but never got ahead, who looked at Simon with envy and always wanted something from him. A favor, a job, money.

The driver came around and opened his door. Cold air swept into the car. "We're pretty casual around here. Without that tie you'll loosen up, maybe enjoy a glass of eggnog."

Their eyes met. Simon identified interest in her gaze, which surprised him along with something else...a heartrending defenselessness. She'd want standing dates on Friday nights, Sunday brunch with her family, midweek lunches. She wasn't his type at all.

"It might make this time of year easier for you if you loosened up," she said.

"I dress for dinner."

She looked Simon up and down, then stepped back to let him out. "*Suit* yourself."

Beneath the clear, starry sky, it was bitingly cold. Even though she toughed the weather in her white cotton shirt, Simon shrugged into his overcoat and grabbed his briefcase.

"You're going to work during Christmas

Eve dinner?" She shut the door behind him and locked the car with a beep of the remote. She was tall and slender, moving with a grace he wouldn't have expected in someone of her profession.

Simon stiffened. What was wrong with him? "I don't go anywhere without my briefcase. If someone calls and I don't have it, I'm screwed." Did he have to choose that particular word? It had been months since he'd been with a woman. Tonight it seemed like years.

His driver demurely looked away.

They walked down the sidewalk toward a house bright with strands of colored lights. A spotlighted manger scene took center stage on the snow-covered lawn, and a huge star outlined in white lights graced the roof. The rumble of voices, laughter and music filled the air. This wasn't a small family gathering. This was a large party.

The cement in the front walk was cracked and uneven—and oddly familiar. Simon slowed his steps. He'd left this all behind. He was Simon Castle, damn it. He wasn't the social misfit anymore and he didn't need anyone wiggling beneath his defenses.

His driver didn't knock when she got to

the door. She just opened it and stepped inside, leaving Simon no choice but to follow.

Kids were everywhere. Small ones played with push cars on the floor. Larger ones darted in and out of the crowd. Teenagers circled around a computer in one corner. The adults looked like the kind of people who lost money they couldn't afford to in his casino, the men dressed in cotton T-shirts and flannel, the women in bright red sweaters decorated with reindeer and snowflakes. They were all packing boxes and wrapping packages. The living room and the dining room beyond it were a flurry of activity.

Everyone seemed to pause when they came in as if they recognized him.

And then there was a wave of excitement…directed at his driver.

"Emma!"

"Em!"

"Emma's here!"

Simon hadn't even known her name.

No one paid any attention to him in their rush to embrace Emma and pull her farther inside the house—which was as hot as a furnace if you were wearing a suit, tie and overcoat. Simon closed the front door and stood awkwardly in the small foyer. No one came to take his coat. No one placed a drink in his hand, although he could see people were drinking. Pink wine and cans of domestic beer. This wasn't his kind of thing at all. A girl ran past him singing.

Six geese a laying...

Looking through the boisterous crowd, trying to figure out what to do next, his eyes fell on the faded red felt stockings trimmed in white hanging from the fireplace, and he froze.

Mom was so sick... It was up to Simon to make sure Santa didn't forget them, so he climbed into the attic to get the Christmas box and arranged her favorite Twelve Days of Christmas figurines on the coffee table. Then he hung his stocking from the wire hook over the mantel.

"What in the hell are you doing?" his father bellowed when he returned from work. "Don't you realize your mother is dying? I'm breaking my back here trying to keep a roof over our heads, and you want a toy?" His dad ripped the stocking from the mantel and tossed it into the cold fireplace. Later that night, Simon carefully pulled it out of the ashes and hung it back up.

A wave of laughter brought Simon back to the present. He was fingering a stocking, standing next to the fire and was warmer than ever now.

CHAPTER FOUR

"MOMMA, YOU HAVE TO COME into the living room." Emma snatched a sugar cookie still hot from the oven and then tugged her mother's arm. "I've never met anyone without an ounce of appreciation for the meaning of Christmas."

The room was warm and smelled of freshly baked cookies ready to be delivered to Santa Express families. Cookie sheets loaded with festive doughy cutouts lined the counter, ready to go into the oven. Round tins were stacked high in the breakfast nook waiting to be filled. Her mother insisted the cookies be baked the day of delivery, even though it overheated the kitchen, using that as an excuse to get out of cooking dinner for fifty people. The dishes laid out in the dining room were potluck.

"Did you bring home another stray? Just like your father, I swear," Donna Roberts said. "Every holiday it's the same thing. One year it was a dog that bit you, another time it was a turtle that wouldn't come out of its shell. What are you going to bring home next?"

"She brought home a *man*." Emma's older brother, Owen, grinned as he took out another tray of cookies. For most of the year, Owen and his buddy, Doc, fought wildland forest fires. But get Owen in a kitchen and he transformed into a woman's dream. To the disappointment of the single women in Virginia City, though, Owen had no interest in settling down.

"A man…" Emma's mother removed her apron and set it on the counter. "Let's meet this man of yours."

"He's not mine," Emma protested, but her mother was off and running. Emma followed her into the living room, where she caught sight of Mr. Castle near the fireplace. He looked about as uncomfortable as a person could be.

"Oh, my goodness. Let's get you out of this coat. Where did you come from? I hope not a funeral." Emma's mother babbled as she bore down on him, grabbing the collar of his overcoat and pulling it down to his elbows.

Emma tried to stop her mother. "Slow down, Momma. He might want to keep that on."

"Nonsense, Emma. Look at him. He's sweating." Emma's mother yanked Mr. Castle's overcoat off the rest of the way. "You went to early church service, didn't you? You must have gone directly from work, and never had a chance to change. But you don't have to worry about that here. It's come as you are at the Robertses' house." Yep, Emma's mom was on a roll. Mr. Castle didn't stand a chance. "We'll just get you settled with a plate, and then you can help pack up boxes for the Express." In less than a minute, Emma's mother had taken Mr. Castle's overcoat and briefcase.

A blank expression on his face, Mr. Castle watched her retreat down the hallway with his things. "What just happened?"

"You'll get used to it." Although it was ten times better to witness it than to be on the receiving end of Momma's whirlwind touch.

Mr. Castle frowned. "I won't be here that long."

Emma was about to explain that time didn't seem to matter where her mother was concerned when Momma returned.

"I do so apologize that I didn't introduce myself. I'm Donna Roberts, Emma's mother." Her faded blue eyes sparkled. "I'm so pleased to meet you...?"

"Castle. Simon Castle."

"Simon," Emma's mother said as Emma rolled the name around her head. It fit the young entrepreneur—classy, cool, distant. "Have you eaten? I'm sure Emma told you that we don't sit down to dinner on Christmas Eve—there's just too much to do. But we do have a large buffet to choose from."

And that's all it took to thaw Simon Castle's cool facade—food.

SIMON LET HIMSELF BE LED to the dining room, where the table was covered with cans of all shapes and sizes—hams, green beans, yams, cranberry sauce. Pairs of adults rotated around the table, one person with a cardboard box, the other loading food into it.

The sideboard was against one wall, laden with platters of nearly demolished piles of food. In the blink of an eye, Simon and Emma had plates in their hands and Donna Roberts fluttered off to wreak havoc with someone else.

"Is she always like that?"

Emma's cheeks were bright pink and her lips twitched suspiciously as she leaned close to him, reaching for the dish of mashed potatoes. "Sometimes she's worse."

"She won't take me by surprise next time," Simon vowed, looking away, toward the sliced ham. He wished he could guard against the surprising effect Emma had on him. He should ignore the unwelcome, growing sense that she needed protection—from *him*—and set the tone for what he wanted once his business in Las Vegas was done—her.

A couple of men in flannel shirts walked by, carrying loaded boxes.

"Lingering under the mistletoe, Em? You know that's an open invitation." The guy with a receding hairline glanced at a sprig of mistletoe taped to a section of ceiling fan before leaning over to kiss Emma's cheek.

Possessiveness gripped Simon and he had to remember to breathe.

The man gave Simon a dismissive once-over and then said to Emma, "Did you hit the guy up for a donation to the Santa Express?"

Simon stiffened. He'd expected this kind of

reception. "I only support *legitimate* charities."

That elicited a frigid smile from the soon-to-be baldy. "Hey, they're all tax deductible and that's what's important to a guy like you this time of year, isn't it?"

"How's the ride, Em?" the other man asked, stepping between Simon and the smart ass, clearly trying to defuse the growing tension. "Should we load up your car for a run?"

"No. I've got work." Emma bobbed her head in Simon's direction.

For some reason, Simon was riled that she'd dismissed him as work. The question was: why? He slapped a dill pickle onto his plate and jostled past the three toward the mashed potatoes.

Five golden ri-i-ings—ba-da-baba...

Some kids joined in the song blasting out of the stereo, mutilating it during the fast countdown. Had Simon ever been that carefree? Would he ever be again? With effort, Simon concentrated on filling his plate. He was losing focus. Las Vegas was important. Eating to keep up his strength was necessary. Superfluous romantic fantasies would only slow him down.

Ignoring Emma, the music and the singers, Simon found a place to sit next to a Christmas tree choked with tinsel and decorations that didn't match, and started eating. The food may have been cold, but it was good, even the yams slathered with marshmallows. He hadn't had yams like that in ages.

"It's good to see you have an appetite," Emma observed, sitting next to him on the sofa. Her plate was nearly as empty as his. "I was beginning to wonder if you worked 24/7, drank power meals and never slept."

"Sleep is highly overrated," he finally managed to say. Simon liked women, had always been good at flirting. But he'd never had a problem putting his wants on hold until his business was done. The attraction he felt for Emma was different. Her smile touched him, demanding he notice her, think about her, push his priorities aside.

"Work is overrated, too," she said.

"Work is everything to me." It was all he had. "I'd expect that from someone without ambition, but you seem bright enough to have gone to college and made something more of yourself. Why would you settle?"

"Is that your idea of a compliment?" Her

eyes flashed. "I own my own business and I make enough to help others, too. We didn't have money for college. But I wouldn't expect you to understand what it's like to lose a parent, or to know how hard it is to be brave for the rest of the family and carry on a father's traditions."

Simon sat back. His mind filled with questions. How? When? Did she still find it hard to sleep at night? His mother had been like Mrs. Roberts before she'd gotten sick. Back then the house had always smelled of good things…like fresh baking and pot roast. After she'd died, it had just smelled dusty.

"My family is busy." Emma stood. "The sooner I get you out of here, the sooner I'll be able to get back."

"And this Express charity? That's done tonight?" He should be jumping up to leave. Instead, he was toying with the idea of telling her he'd lost someone, too.

"All deliveries are tonight. Over one hundred needy families will have a merrier Christmas thanks to the work of the folks here." She reached for his plate. "It would be great if I could stay and help."

His brain reawakened. "I'm paying you to

get me to Vegas, not waste time on frivolous charities."

She froze, her hand above his plate. "Frivolous—"

"People come to expect handouts," Simon cut her off, hearing his father's voice as he spoke. "I'd never take someone's charity. I've always made my own way."

Her eyes blazed as she captured the rim of his plate. "Sometimes you don't have a choice. Everyone here knows that and wants to help." Emma tried to yank the dish from him.

"People who build their own destiny don't believe in charity or a free lunch." He didn't let go of the plate. For some unknown reason, it was important that she agree with him. "The only person you should rely on is you. A fare like mine should go into your savings so you can buy a second car and hire another driver, grow your business. But I expect you'll be giving it away."

"Since there's no free lunch, we'll accept your fifty-dollar donation for dinner," she said, pointedly ignoring his business advice.

"Mister, can you help me wrap this?" A sturdy young boy interrupted them, his shirt tail hanging over his rumpled jeans as he juggled a roll of wrapping paper, tape and a Yahtzee game. "I'd ask Aunt Emma, but she's a girl and I don't ask girls for anything."

Simon was so startled, he let the plate go, allowing Emma to escape to the kitchen.

With dramatic eye-rolling, the kid dumped his items on the couch next to Simon. "My name's Johnny. The quicker we wrap, the sooner we can have pie. Do you know how to wrap? If not, I need to go find someone else." He glanced around the room and Simon followed his lead, taking in all the blue-collar dads and uncles who fit in so well. "My dad's busy and all the good uncles are taken." Johnny turned back to Simon, sizing him up. Based on his frown, he wasn't impressed with what he saw.

"So, you're in this for the pie?" What would Emma say about good deeds and intention if she heard that?

"Aren't you?"

Two giggling girls ran by with tinsel in their hair, twirling empty wrapping paper rolls like batons. Johnny frowned at them, too.

It had been years since Simon wrapped

anything. After his mom had died, he and his dad had tried their best to avoid this holiday.

Nevertheless, feeling the boy's eyes on him, Simon began rolling out the paper.

"Grandma's pies are the best." Johnny smacked his lips. "My new best friend, Wallace, he's really good with music, but his mom has to spend money on the doctor bills instead of presents this year. I put his name on the Express list because I don't want Wallace to be sad."

Okay, so maybe Emma was right. Even the kid wanted to help for reasons other than a slice of pie. As Simon wrapped the Yahtzee box, he couldn't remember ever being as caring as this little boy. He'd been too lost in his own pain.

"IT'S NOT OFTEN YOU FIND someone so excited about Christmas," Emma's mom said as she bustled into the kitchen with a load of dirty dinner plates.

"Particularly a CEO," Owen added, following with more dishes.

"You can't be talking about Simon Castle. In his opinion, the Santa Express is *frivolous*." Emma ripped off a piece of wax paper with a bit too much gusto and worked it into place in a cookie tin. He didn't care that Emma was going to break Momma's heart when she told her they had to leave.

Owen scraped food off the dirty dishes. "You could have fooled me the way he and Johnny are race-wrapping Doc and Teddy."

"The sooner he's done..." Emma couldn't tell her mother she was leaving yet. And then, to her horror, Emma's voice cracked as she blurted, "I really blew it this time."

"What's wrong?" her mom asked, putting her arm around Emma. "You're with family. It's the holiday—"

"And you own a nice car," Owen said. "Ow! What'd I do?" he said when their mother poked him in the ribs.

"Money can't guarantee happiness," Momma admonished Owen, then turned to Emma. "Do you need money, Em?"

The thick bulge of cash in her pants pocket felt as noticeable as a third appendage. "I don't need money."

"Did the CEO get you pregnant?" With a scowl, Owen took a step toward the kitchen doorway.

"No!" Emma grabbed a handful of Owen's flannel shirt and pulled him back. "It all started so innocently," Emma tried to explain. "I was dropping off a fare, fully intending to come straight home when along comes Mr. Castle and he wouldn't get out of my car." She paused to catch her breath, knowing what she needed to say, yet unable to confess she'd have to leave soon. "I've never met anyone so driven. He thinks he's on the brink of getting the perfect life." He was the perfect challenge, and she was surprised to realize that she was attracted to the compelling mix of regret and longing in his eyes.

With an expression that said his sister was nuts, Owen opened the door a crack, presumably to get a better look at Simon.

"Now, Emma," her mother began with that stern expression of hers. "I knew it would come to this someday. You can't *make* somebody believe in the same things you do. You'll end up getting hurt."

Emma turned back to the cookie tin to hide the blush heating her cheeks. "Simon Castle is as cold and uncaring as the rat in his parking lot."

"I don't know about any hotel rats, but I think you're losing it." Owen had always been good at spying when they were kids. "Come here and take a look. He's laughing."

Sure enough, when Emma peeked out, she would have sworn Simon and Johnny were having the time of their lives.

"That doesn't count," Simon challenged Doc, gesturing wildly at a large package. "It's too ugly. I'd be embarrassed to give it to someone."

Emma couldn't believe what she saw. Simon's hair was rumpled and he had a piece of tape on his tie. He sat surrounded by sloppily wrapped gifts.

"It's a work of modern art," Doc protested, his glasses slipping to the end of his nose as he held up the oblong, knobby package wrapped in red-and-green Grinch paper.

Simon scoffed. "But your paper is so cockeyed, you can see what the present is through the seams."

There were calls from the crowd to rewrap. Doc reluctantly tore off the paper from the piano keyboard and started again. Meanwhile, Simon charged toward the kitchen, scattering the three Robertses away from the door.

"We need more tape," Simon said as he barged in and held out his hands imploringly to Emma's mother. "Tape?"

Emma couldn't help but laugh. Owen was right. Simon did have the Christmas spirit. Surely, he'd let Emma stay and help with Santa Express deliveries, and admit there was joy in the season. She wanted to hug someone and shout, "Merry Christmas!"

Introducing himself, Owen shook hands with Simon.

Emma's mother produced a handful of tape rolls from the junk drawer. "I bet we're running out all over the house," she said, hurrying over with the dispensers.

Johnny poked his head into the kitchen. "Mister, come on. They're almost done re-wrapping that keyboard."

"Three more presents and we'll be crowned the winner!" Simon pointed at Emma with a tape roll. "Then we're off to Vegas."

"Bit of a competitive streak?" Owen looked from the swinging kitchen door to Emma, and then uncomfortably away as he realized what he'd said.

Simon Castle was competitive, not excited about Christmas.

Emma sighed. "A small competitive streak." Only about a mile wide. That, and an apparent obsession with money, would guarantee Simon a lonely holiday.

"What did he mean 'off to Vegas?'" Momma crossed her arms over her chest.

"You're eloping to Vegas? I thought you didn't like the guy." Owen stood next to Momma and crossed his arms as well.

"No." Emma's cheeks heated. "I've been trying to tell you that I can't stay. I'm driving Mr. Castle to Vegas tonight."

"You took a job on Christmas." Momma sank into a chair. "Why?"

"Is he getting a kidney transplant in the morning? It must be important for you to blow off the Express." Owen brought Momma a glass of water.

"I...uh..." Emma thrust her hands into her back pockets, away from Mr. Castle's money. "He has an important business meeting tomorrow."

"On Christmas?" Owen didn't hide his disdain. "Are you sure he doesn't have a hot date with a showgirl?"

"Hey, this is one of those make-it or break-it business meetings."

"Stop it, you two," Momma commanded. "There will be other Christmases together, but for now we've got to get through this one."

CHAPTER FIVE

"WE MAKE A GOOD TEAM, KID. When you graduate from college come see me." Simon patted Johnny on the head. He couldn't remember the last time he'd had so much fun, and all he'd done was won a gift-wrapping race. He couldn't wait to get on the road to Vegas. Luck was with him tonight. Hopefully, it would carry through until morning.

"I'm not a dog, Mister." Johnny brushed Simon's hand away. "You high five when you do a good job." He held up his hand until Simon gave him five. "Why do I need to come see you?"

"For a job."

"Jeez, I'm only eight. I'm too young to go to work." Shaking his head, Johnny disappeared into the sea of kids, leaving Simon standing awkward and alone.

"Congratulations. You're the best wrapper

I've been up against in years." The young man they called Doc thrust his hand at Simon. "I'm Owen's friend, Jordan Donato. Most people call me Doc."

Simon introduced himself.

"The Robertses know how to make giving a party." Doc knelt and gathered wrapping odds and ends off the floor. "Is this your first time?"

"Hard to tell, I know." Simon reached to help him. "And you come every year?"

"Wouldn't miss it. The food's great and the beer's free, although we only get one until we finish deliveries. And the women love us."

Simon handed Doc the crumpled remains of their efforts. He noticed Johnny in between stacks of cans at the dining room table, eating a piece of pie loaded with whipped cream.

"You know—" Doc lowered his voice "—you've been looking at everyone here as if we're members of a cult or something. We're just a big group of friends lucky enough to be able to give something to people less fortunate."

Emma's brother, Owen, appeared in front of them with a clipboard. "Doc, you brought your truck, right?" When Doc nodded, he turned to Simon with a determined set to his brow. "We need one more vehicle and another pair of hands."

"Don't even think about it." Simon had more important things to do than act as a delivery boy. "I've got to be in Vegas in…" He glanced at his watch. "Eleven hours. And Emma's agreed to drive me." No way was she stranding him in Virginia City for this.

Owen exchanged a glance with Doc, then indicated they should sit on the couch next to the Christmas tree. "We treat everyone who enters our door on Christmas Eve like family, so I'm going to be blunt."

"Good, because neither one of us has time for anything less."

"You won't get anywhere with Emma if you consider money more important than people," Owen pointed out.

Simon bristled. "The only place I want to get with Emma is Vegas so I can attend a very important business meeting." Somehow he'd overlooked Owen's attack on his character in his haste to deny the attraction between him and Emma.

Doc laughed. "You're going to a meeting? On Christmas Day? What kind of people have a business meeting on Christmas?"

"The kind you and I wouldn't consider doing business with," Owen answered Doc slowly. "I know Emma agreed to drive you to Vegas, but she looks at you as if she was digging through her stocking on Christmas morning."

Simon could picture Emma on the floor with a stocking in her lap, her eyes sparkling as she discovered one small treasure after another. He tried to recall seeing that joy on Emma's face when she looked at him, but couldn't.... But he felt something unfamiliar, distinctly close to male pride, at the thought.

"Emma loves the Santa Express and everyone here loves Emma," Owen added, just in case Simon was a numskull. "We don't want to see her fall for the wrong guy and get hurt."

Simon saw Emma put her arms around Johnny and give him a tender squeeze. Simon couldn't believe it—he actually felt jealous of the kid.

"Emma drove you here, right? You might want to check with her before you turn us down if you want whatever you've got going to last beyond tonight—business or otherwise."

"Nothing is going on between us." Simon scowled, even as he couldn't take his eyes off Emma clearing dessert dishes from the dining-room table.

His denial only made Doc laugh again. "Dude, all I'm saying is it's Christmas. Count your blessings and don't take someone like Emma for granted. You never know when your luck will change."

Doc and Owen left Simon, who continued to deny his attraction to Emma even after they were out of sight.

Someone snorted on the floor next to Simon and he glanced down. A drooling toddler with a pile of ornaments at his feet grinned up at him. Then the child turned to the Christmas tree and took another ornament off, placed it with a clink on his pile of sparkly goods and snorted again.

"I don't think these are supposed to be on the floor." Simon bent and picked up a pink plastic rocking horse and a red glass ball, returning them to the nearest bare spots on the tree he could find. Next to one of them, a Popsicle-stick picture-frame ornament caught his eye. It was a picture of a smiling girl with braces who looked just like Emma might have at about twelve.

Simon leaned in for a closer look. His school pictures had been stiff and bland. In hers, she looked open, trusting, ready for anything life sent her way. Simon couldn't keep from smiling.

The tyrant on the floor let out a shriek louder than a siren that wiped the smile from Simon's face. He looked around, half expecting a mother in a knit sweater to descend upon him as if he were the Grinch himself.

A redheaded girl was immediately at Simon's side. "Garrett, no, no, no. The orn'ments go on the tree, remember?" She began putting things back.

Garrett made a keening sound and then he shrieked again, his entire body rigid.

"I didn't touch him," Simon said to no one in particular, wishing someone would make the kid stop.

"Don't you want the tree to be pretty, Garrett?" the girl crooned, bending to pick up more ornaments.

Drooly-boy reached nearly glass-shattering pitch. Still, there was no sign of his mother.

"I don't think he likes that," Simon leaned over to shout in the girl's ear.

She ignored him and kept putting ornaments back. "Orn'ments go on Christmas trees." As efficient as Simon could hope for in an employee, she got them all back and then skipped off.

The screaming stopped with a shuddering gasp. Garrett exchanged a long sad look with Simon. Huge crocodile tears tumbled down the toddler's red cheeks. Without thinking, Simon handed the boy the plastic rocking horse.

Garrett stared at it for a moment, clutching it in his fist. He stood on his wobbly legs and then took another ornament off the tree. With a wheezy laugh, the kid placed both at his feet.

The toddler reached for Emma's Popsicle picture, but Simon was quicker, moving her ornament to a safer location higher up. Garrett gave a halfhearted wail, but settled on a nearby ribbon-and-lace angel instead. It wasn't going to take long for him to accumulate another pile. Suspecting the house was in for another screech-fest as soon as the bossy little girl discovered what Garrett was up to, Simon went in search of Emma.

It was time to get back to business.

"MISS ROBERTS?" The woman's voice wasn't familiar.

Emma pressed her cell phone closer to her ear. "Yes."

"This is Marlene, Mr. Castle's secretary." The woman in the wheelchair. "I'm just checking on your progress. Is everything okay?"

"Fine." If you considered ankle-high spirits fine.

"And you'll arrive in time for the meeting?" Worry tinged Marlene's voice.

"Marlene, please enjoy your Christmas. I'll get Mr. Castle where he needs to be." Emma disconnected and put the small phone in her belt clip before returning to the dirty dishes.

"It's getting to be *that time*," Momma announced, plopping a Santa hat onto Emma's head. "We need to load up the sleighs."

Emma dried her hands. She knew Momma wouldn't give up on her so easily. "I've got to take Mr. Castle to Las Vegas tonight."

"He's such a nice man." Emma's mother ignored the ringing telephone. "And it's Christmas Eve. Surely you can ask Mr. Castle to postpone?"

"No. I took the job knowing what I had to

do." With a sinking heart, Emma pulled off her hat and reached for the folded bills in her pocket. Even the thought of giving the money to those less fortunate wasn't salve to the guilt she felt for disappointing her family.

Excited male voices began shouting, "Let's go! Hurry!"

Doc burst into the kitchen. "Sorry, ladies. There's a fire at a house south of town. I'm taking the volunteer firemen, including Owen." He gave Emma's mom a handful of car keys and a clipboard. "These are the trucks we've loaded so far and the list of deliveries."

"You can't all leave," Emma protested. There had to be at least eight firefighters in the house…rapidly leaving by the sound of things. "What are we going to do without you?"

"Whatever happened to women who don't need men?" Doc was already heading toward the door, salivating to get to a fire.

With near the same level of enthusiasm, Owen gave his mother a quick kiss. "Mom, you can handle it."

"No." Emma blocked Owen's path.

"Oh, let them go, Emma." Momma splayed the keys on the counter.

"But we won't have enough drivers," Emma said. "We're not done filling the cookie tins. Besides, who'll stay with the kids if we go?"

"The CEO," Owen said, backing out and into Simon, who carried a small piece of pumpkin pie. "We have every member of the volunteer fire department here, plus some. Putting out the fire should be a snap."

"The *CEO* is not a babysitter." Simon bristled. "The CEO needs to be in Las Vegas."

Owen apologized. Horns honked outside. "You'll sort it out, Em. Gotta go."

"It's almost seven o'clock." The Santa hat lay crumpled on the counter. Emma's fingers twitched. "More than one hundred families and six drivers? We'll be delivering until midnight without help."

"Not *we'll* be delivering, *they'll* be delivering, as in without you and me." Simon waved a hand in front of her face. "I hired you to drive me to Las Vegas. Can we go now?"

His attitude fired a single-minded purpose in Emma that had been lacking earlier. Snatching the hat from the counter, Emma jammed it on her head. Her father would never have let the community down. "No. I'll get you to Vegas in time for your meeting. I just need a couple of hours here."

"That's not—"

"This is not negotiable, Mr. Castle." She turned away from him and the deal she'd made. "Momma, we'll have the high-school kids bake, and you and I can make deliveries." Emma picked up the clipboard and scanned it.

"Of course, dear." Emma's mother glanced at Simon with a smile meant to charm. Emma doubted it would have any effect on Simon. "I'll go see if they're ready to load up."

"You—" Emma pointed at Simon without letting him get a word in "—go sit in a corner, eat your pie and check your strawberry for messages."

"BlackBerry," he corrected, a stormy angle to his brows. "I brought the pie for you, but neither one of us has time—"

"You have all the time in the world." Emma ignored the way his pie offering warmed her. "But if I don't get these presents out of here soon, there will be kids who won't have anything to eat on Christmas, much less a toy to play with."

Momma cradled the keys in both hands. "It shouldn't be so hard. We've got four trucks loaded and the cookie tins are nearly full."

Simon followed so close, he almost bumped into Emma as she entered the dining room. "But—"

"No buts. Sit." Emma pointed to a corner chair in the living room before grabbing an empty box and starting to fill it.

CHAPTER SIX

PLEASE CONFIRM YOUR attendance upon arrival. Erik Wiseman.

Didn't Maloof's assistant ever take a break? His brief e-mail sent Simon's blood pressure soaring. He was trapped in Virginia City. The meeting would go on without him. Most likely, Maloof wouldn't even realize Simon wasn't there.

Fuming, Simon sat where he had a clear view of the lopsided, overdecorated tree, a sappy holiday movie on the TV and Emma flailing about the dining room trying to organize the women and teenagers. Emma was a beacon among them, with her fiery hair and high energy. The efforts of the remaining volunteers were lackluster, their enthusiasm drained since the men had left. Emma's charity was as doomed as Simon's desire to be in Las Vegas.

Simon stroked his BlackBerry. This

Christmas was turning out to be among the worst ever. Rats. Limo drivers who refused to drive. What else could go wrong?

"Who works on Christmas?" he heard someone say. "Do you see him over there? He could be helping."

"If you were the head of a large corporation, you'd probably work every day of the year, too," Emma said defensively, dodging a kid who bumped the box she was carrying. "All right. That's it. Everyone under twelve needs to go out to the living room and *sit.*"

A local newscaster appeared on the television screen, catching Simon's attention. "Who is the Rat of Reno? Tune in at eleven to learn why Simon Castle, founder and CEO of Castle Hotels, has riled employees once more and won't be having a merry Christmas." They flashed a picture of the large sharp-clawed rat in Simon's parking lot on-screen with the hotel logo looming behind it.

If blood could boil…

The couch cushion bounced next to him. "Mom said I was too small to help." Johnny pouted. "Aunt Emma said to come sit over here with the babysitter."

Simon glanced around the room filling

with children. His quiet corner was fast disappearing. He waited for an adult or teenager—the babysitter—to come in, but he was the only one in the room older than ten. *He* was the babysitter.

"That's just not right," Simon said under his breath.

A glance showed the chaos whirling about Emma. She was really no good at organizing. He suspected she'd be better watching over these kids than he would.

Someone sneezed, followed by an eruption of loud *eeewwws!*

"Tommy, get a tissue!"

"He got some on me!"

"Hey, don't push me. I didn't sneeze on you."

Scowling eyes swiveled from Tommy, another toddler, to Simon. Boogers were something a babysitter was supposed to take care of. When Simon didn't, the kids rose in anger. Someone would have to be sacrificed, most likely Tommy-boy.

Simon had a choice: tackle the Booger Riot or participate in the chaos of Christmas, charity and ho-ho-hos.

Another juicy sneeze. Another chorus of *eeewww.*

"Come on, kid. This isn't the room for us." He dragged Johnny through the raucous group toward the dining room. Maybe the fire would be put out quickly, the men would return and Simon would get out of here and make the meeting. Maybe the networks wouldn't pick up the rat story. And maybe there was a Santa Claus.

"Becky, I need you and Brian to take the south end of town. It's got the heaviest boxes," Emma was saying.

"But I have the smallest car," Becky argued.

"Emma—" a teenage boy popped his head in from the kitchen "—we burned a batch of cookies."

"Do we have any more boxes? I think we're out of boxes," announced a woman with wild gray hair.

"Look at the time," pointed out an older woman wearing a sweatshirt with a holly wreath made out of children's handprints. "We're never going to make it without the guys. And our own Christmas will be ruined. Why don't we wait until morning to deliver this stuff, when the guys get back?"

"We can do this, Dora," Emma countered in a panicked voice. "Once you see the smiles and hear the thank yous, you won't feel as if your holiday is ruined."

A few of the women muttered, and Simon sensed impending disaster. His pulse raced and, for the first time all evening, Simon felt at home. He thrived on crisis management.

He couldn't resist leaning close to Emma and whispering in her ear, "What happened to merry Christmas and the joy of helping others?" She smelled like cinnamon and spice. Simon breathed in a second time before he realized what he was doing and pulled back.

"We've never had to do this by ourselves before," Emma said with a frown in Simon's direction. "We're short-staffed."

"You didn't have a backup plan?" Simon raised his eyebrows.

"It's a charity, not a business," Emma snapped back. "Next thing, you'll be wondering if we have insurance to cover our drivers."

Simon waved her off. "Organize. Cover contingencies. Plan for the future the same as you would your own life. Nobody watches out for you better than you. That's common sense, not business." Emma opened her mouth to retort, but Simon cut her off. "Show me the list of delivery locations, and you—" he pointed to Becky "—make a list of available vehicles. And you—" he took Dora, the mutinous woman, by the arm and pointed her in the direction of the living room where empty rolls of wrapping paper were being wielding like swords "—can watch the kids."

Simon poked his head in the kitchen where two teenagers were kissing under the mistletoe hanging from the outdated light fixture. "Quit messing around and set the timer. If you can't handle that, Tommy needs help blowing his nose in the living room." He waited until the teens moved to the oven before leaving them alone again.

"You're helping us?" The disbelief on Emma's face should have irritated Simon.

Instead, he laughed. "At the rate you're going, we'll never get out of here tonight."

"We've just hit a rough patch," Emma assured him, ruffled. "You'll get to Vegas in plenty of time."

"Yes, I will." He was going to make sure of it, if he had to make every delivery for the Santa Express himself. "Now, what's this I hear about a box shortage?"

"THAT MR. CASTLE IS a miracle worker," Momma said, clearly charmed. "What does he do for a living?"

"He owns Castle Hotels." Emma had to agree that Simon was a blessing in disguise. He'd taken the bedlam and mutiny and co-ordinated the volunteers into something resembling a team. He'd organized a group to repack donations for the smaller families into bags so that there were enough boxes to go around. The vehicles were divvied up as well, with one adult and one teen in each. The smaller vehicles held the smaller donations, the trucks and larger cars, like Emma's Town Car, the larger ones. As far as Emma could see, there was just one problem.

"You and I are going together?" she asked again when he passed her way.

Simon nodded, reviewing a list of destinations he'd assigned someone else to write down. Emma followed him through the dining room to the kitchen. "And when we're done, you and I are going to Vegas." He paused in the doorway, one hand on the swinging door.

"You're under the mistletoe, dears," Emma's mom noted with a twinkle in her eye. "You know what that means."

Emma froze, her gaze meeting Simon's. *Say something, stupid.*

To her complete surprise, Simon leaned over and pressed his lips to hers.

Something warm flickered inside Emma, making her want to curl her fingers around Simon's arms and pull him closer. Instead, she stumbled back into the door frame, bumping her head and seeing stars around Simon's face.

"I don't normally have that effect on women," he said, closing the distance between them and running his fingers through her hair as he searched for a bruise.

"I bet you don't normally kiss them under the mistletoe, either." Emma was still too unsteady to trust herself to step away. Who would have thought the unfeeling Simon Castle could generate such feelings in her?

Who was she kidding? She'd wanted him from the moment she'd laid eyes on him in her rearview mirror.

"Gosh, if you marry my aunt Emma, you can help with the Santa Express every year," Johnny piped up from the dining room.

Cheeks heating, Emma slipped away to retrieve her car keys. She didn't dare look at Simon. This was not the kind of holiday cheer she should be spreading to her client. She groaned. She had to endure eight hours alone in the car with Simon. Maybe he'd sleep on the way to Las Vegas—*all* the way to Las Vegas.

AS SIMON WATCHED HER WALK AWAY, he could no longer deny he wanted Emma Roberts. If only the feeling wasn't so inconvenient. After tonight, they'd go their separate ways and she'd annoy another unsuspecting passenger.

Someone tugged on his hand. "Are you?"

Simon looked down in confusion at his temporary administrative assistant, Johnny. "Am I what?"

Johnny rolled his big blue eyes dramatically. "Going to marry Aunt Emma?"

Laughter erupted all around them, even though the work didn't stop. When they were organized, they were an efficient group. Simon wished his employees were that motivated.

Unable to keep from grinning, Simon checked his watch. "This convoy leaves in ten minutes."

"So, the businessman has a heart after all," someone said behind him.

"Everyone has a heart on Christmas," Mrs. Roberts said staunchly, sending Simon an approving look the likes he hadn't seen since his mother was alive.

CHAPTER SEVEN

"TWELVE STOPS AND THEN WE'RE on our way," Simon said, settling into the front seat next to Emma with no indication that he was uncomfortable after their earlier kiss.

Emma couldn't forget it. She'd been counting on Simon sitting in the backseat—keeping his distance.

Without a word—because she couldn't trust herself to speak—Emma drove toward the first stop, a family of five living in a one-bedroom house behind a grocery store.

"How long do you think this will take?" Simon asked, glancing at his BlackBerry, although he didn't work the keys. He'd barely seemed to notice the sights as they'd crossed the center of town.

"Maybe two hours." Emma braced herself for Simon's reaction, which was likely to be colder and more furious than a blizzard.

"And how long to Las Vegas from here?"

"Eight." Barring any snow, accidents or slow drivers, they'd just make it.

Amazing. The blizzard held off.

"It looked as if you were having fun wrapping with Johnny," Emma ventured.

"He's a good kid," Simon allowed. "Was his dad there?"

"Yes. Gerry's the one who looks like a linebacker. He married my cousin, Kate."

"They all look like linebackers."

"Oh." Emma supposed a stranger would look at all the firemen that way. "He's the balding linebacker."

"Ah." Simon checked his BlackBerry again. "I'm sorry you lost your dad. What happened to him?" The question may have been casual, but Emma could feel his scrutiny.

"He was killed," she said.

"I'm sorry." His touch on her shoulder was so brief, she almost thought she'd imagined it. "How did he die?"

Emma spared him a glance, gauging the emotion behind his request. The look in his eyes wasn't polite pity as she so often saw, but curiosity and perhaps… understanding. "My dad was a professor of sociology at the university in Reno. He was studying the impact of America's increasing inner focus as it related to the Christmas holiday."

"Can you say that again in earth-speak?"

Emma almost smiled. "My dad noticed that fewer people were sending Christmas cards, baking cookies, buying real Christmas trees, hosting holiday parties and such. He thought it was becoming something else to add to our to-do list rather than a time to reflect on traditions and enjoy the relationships you have, which translates into more stress, shorter tempers and contributes to health problems."

"That explains a lot about you," he said, "but not how he died."

"He was mugged." It was ten years later, and Emma's eyes still filled with tears when she talked about her dad. "He was going door-to-door for his research in some of the poorer sections of Reno the week before Christmas and someone must have thought he was an easy target." She added quickly, "Please don't make a joke of it. I've heard them all." Her dad, killed by Christmas.

"It's not a joking matter." He kept his hand on her shoulder longer this time.

"It's hard to imagine anyone would kill

him for the fifty bucks he had in his wallet. He was such a big, trusting teddy bear of a man."

They pulled onto a street of small rectangular houses lacking even a hint of Christmas decorations.

"You still miss him."

She nodded. "Especially at this time of year."

"Despite that, you'll go out and help others, in neighborhoods like this." Simon gestured to the run-down homes around them.

"Mom, Owen and I decided keeping the Santa Express alive was the best way to honor Dad's memory. He was a real believer in the season and if you gave him two minutes of your time, he could make you a believer, too."

"Like father, like daughter."

It was a good thing Emma had the car in Park because she couldn't tear herself away from the intensity of his gaze. She almost wished the Town Car didn't have such wide seats.

Apparently Simon was thinking the same thing. He slowly leaned toward her and pressed his mouth to hers with a heat that compelled Emma to kiss him back. Lips like his should have a warning label— Caution: May Overheat If Turned on Unattended.

It took Emma a moment to realize his lips had left hers. His palms cradled her face. She held on to his wrists. They stared into each others' eyes in an awkward moment. "Merry Christmas," she finally managed to say, with a tentative smile she hoped said, *Kiss me again.*

"Only if we keep to the schedule, Emma." His words were cool, but his eyes betrayed a longing that matched hers. As they got out of the car, Simon changed the subject. "Do we just leave the packages on the doorstep? The house looks dark."

"That would be quicker, but it's not the way the Santa Express operates. They're expecting us." Okay. If he could play detached, so could she. Kind of. She still had a few surprises for Simon. Emma popped the trunk and pulled out a red hat similar to the one she was wearing. "I can't let you make deliveries without the hat."

Simon stepped back and eyed it as if he were in imminent danger. "You're kidding, right?"

Emma shook her head solemnly. "You can either help or you can wait in the car."

"Which would mean these deliveries would take that much longer." With a frown, Simon snatched the hat. "I'll carry it."

"No go. It sits on your head. I'm willing to wait here all night until it does." Emma crossed her arms over her chest before adding, "With the keys in my hand."

His eyes narrowed, sending a thrill through Emma. "That's blackmail."

"Yep. I've got a reputation to protect." For the first time since she'd met him, she felt as if they were equals.

Simon pulled the hat over his ears and nudged Emma aside so he could reach inside the trunk for a box. This was priceless. The only thing better would be to see the rat outside his hotel in a Santa hat.

"That must be some meeting," Emma observed, grabbing a sack of presents.

"You don't know what it's like to be the outsider, do you?" Simon asked as he headed up the walk, carrying the heavy box with ease.

"I was born an outsider." Emma couldn't quite achieve the note of levity she desired. "You've heard of the glass ceiling? Well, there's also a *class* ceiling. Not everyone is born into money."

"I grew up in a house a lot like this one." Simon's revelation surprised her. He reeked of stiff-backed, old money. "I'm proof that there is no ceiling if you have a goal you're serious about and pursue it relentlessly every day."

"That doesn't sound as if it leaves much room for anything else." Like a wife or a family. Emma stabbed at the doorbell as she juggled the bags of gifts.

"There's not."

Emma's heart sank. What had she been expecting? He'd made himself into a successful businessman. She was, and would probably always be, content with her lifestyle. He'd drawn lines clear enough for Emma to read. There would be no more pursuit of their mutual attraction.

Emma straightened her shoulders. They both needed to lighten up.

"It's too bad you only think about work. Life doesn't wait around, you know." She couldn't resist jostling Simon in the shoulder. "You have to say 'Merry Christmas' when they answer."

Simon made a growling noise.

"And mean it," Emma added as the door opened, turning to muster a smile.

SIMON COULDN'T REMEMBER ANYONE ever being so happy to see him as that first Santa Express family. He deposited the box of food with the fixings for their Christmas dinner on the wobbly kitchen table and was immediately enveloped in a bear hug from the robust lady of the house.

"It was getting so late, we thought you might not be coming," she said wiping away tears when she finally released him. "Merry Christmas."

"You shouldn't have worried. Nothing stops the Santa Express," Simon said, watching as Emma's expression changed from curious to approving.

There was much more to Emma than he'd first expected. She wasn't an overboard, Christmas-loving do-gooder. She was honoring her father. It all made sense now. Emma's heart was larger than Simon's would ever be. Unlike him, she'd never want for friends or family. And the way she kissed—with uninhibited abandon—she wouldn't stay single much longer.

"You can put the gifts under the tree," the

woman said, pointing to a crooked tree that barely stood two feet tall.

The tree was propped on a scarred coffee table. Emma deposited the gifts with a smile that warmed Simon from his fingers to his toes.

A man appeared in the hallway with a baby cradled in one arm and a toddler snuggled in the other. "Both our little ones went down with bronchitis yesterday, so we had a big doctor bill today. Every time I put them down, they cough themselves back awake." He deposited the toddler in his wife's arms and shook Simon's hand with bone-popping strength. "You don't know how much this helps us, especially since I've been laid off. No one's hiring mechanics this time of year."

"Never you mind, Rueben," his wife said. "You'll find a job in the new year." She could have put her husband down, but instead, she was positive and supportive, as if she hadn't been crying with relief just moments before.

The sentiment and encouragement humbled Simon, who would have been bitter if their situations had been reversed. He certainly hadn't been raised with such compassion. Simon remembered his dad complaining when his mother had become so sick she could no longer work. His father's love seemed shallow compared to this couple's. Someone like Emma would offer that kind of love to her partner and expect—no, demand—it be returned in kind.

Simon looked up to find Emma studying him. She turned, spoke softly to the other woman and pressed something into the woman's hands.

"We need to be going." Simon's voice was unexpectedly thick.

"Thank you, thank you." The big man shook Simon's hand again as he tried to leave. "This means so much to us."

"Maybe next year you can help make Santa Express deliveries," Emma suggested, before following Simon out the door.

"I'd love to," the man said. "I'll keep in touch. Merry Christmas!"

Simon and Emma didn't speak until they were back in the car.

"That wasn't what I expected," Simon admitted, an odd emptiness making him restless. He didn't want to sit in the car. He wanted to…do something. Unbidden, a long forgotten memory of his mother humming while she wrapped presents on her bed came to mind. Simon had been trying to stack bows on the floor at her feet when his father had burst into the room, swept Simon's mother into his arms and kissed her. Then he'd lifted Simon with strong arms, holding him so tight Simon didn't think he'd ever let go.

"You thought we'd be dropping in on cold-hearted freeloaders?"

"No. I expected it to be more like the house I grew up in, with a father too proud to accept help. I just…didn't expect them to be so…grateful. I'm sorry." Sorry for thinking the Santa Express wasn't worth his time or money. Sorry he hadn't realized there were more sides to love than he'd known as a child, because now a woman with expectations was tempting him and Simon had no idea how to be the man she'd want.

"In case no one told you, this is the season to spread joy and give thanks," Emma said in a flat voice.

"So you've told me. I just didn't believe it."

"Do you have any family traditions for the holidays?" Emma asked.

The night may have been chilly, but Emma felt warm. Simon was starting to come around. He'd worn the Santa hat all evening and he hadn't mentioned Las Vegas since they'd left the first house—although it helped that the reported fire had been a bonfire so the men had caught up with most of the delivery teams. Doc and Owen had taken half of Emma and Simon's load.

Simon waited so long to answer, Emma didn't think he was going to. "Christmas isn't my favorite time of year. My mother died when I was a kid." He added almost as an afterthought, "Just after the holiday."

She gave Simon's hand a squeeze, surprised as he held on to her fingers when she would have let go. "That's a horrible thing to have to grow up with…or without. A mom, I mean."

"I used to think we got by," he said slowly. "But after seeing these families, I'm beginning to think we were luckier than most. We faced tragedy, but we still had a roof over our heads and food in the kitchen."

"And your dad?"

"We don't see each other much. I think we both like it that way." There was a sadness in his voice that said otherwise. He let go of her hand.

"Are you sure?"

"Does Christmas fall on the twenty-fifth of December? My old man doesn't agree with anything I do. He doesn't care for anyone but himself."

"Really?" This last might have described the world's view of Simon Castle, a view Emma now disagreed with.

He reached for his BlackBerry. "I don't have time to do things like this. I'd rather send money and leave the actual giving to the professionals."

"My dad would have loved talking to you." Emma kept seeing glimpses of Simon that she was attracted to. "It's amazing the things we take for granted, like family and a steady paycheck."

"I don't take anything for granted because I've worked so hard to get here. And I got here without anyone else's help." Maybe he had every right to feel this proud.

Yet, Emma couldn't relate. She put the Town Car in Park and turned to face him. "You never asked for advice? You never got an unexpected break? You say you did it on your own, but I bet someone somewhere along the line helped you. This is your chance to return the favor."

Simon's expression darkened. "I've never said I was anything other than what I am. I'm not like you. I put my goals and needs first."

Emma had to swallow twice before she was able to speak. "Do you ever stop to ask yourself if you're happy?"

"I'm about to achieve more success than I ever imagined."

"That's not an answer." Not the answer Emma wanted. She knew come morning that Simon would disappear through darkened casino doors and she'd drive back to Virginia City alone. Yet, she'd worry about Simon long after he'd forgotten her because somehow that impossibly driven, vulnerable man had found the route to her heart. Her mother had been right. Trying to make someone believe only led to heartache.

Emma opened her door to get out, angry at herself, angry at Simon. "Why don't you spend your time in a more *productive* manner? I can handle this one on my own."

CHAPTER EIGHT

WAS SIMON HAPPY?

Simon hadn't questioned it until now. What did happiness matter when you were making something out of nothing? Simon sat in the car as the heat dissipated. He could hear Emma rummaging in the trunk. He should help her, but he stubbornly remained where he was.

The surface of his BlackBerry was cold. Nothing new had come in since Maloof's assistant's last e-mail. Undoubtedly, everyone Simon dealt with was home stuffing themselves with turkey, yams and pumpkin pie.

Simon had smiled more this evening than he had in a long time. Emma's family, her charity, the arguments with Emma and her wholehearted kisses, all of it chaotic and unpredictable, yet oddly satisfying—a feeling his money and success had been unable to evoke.

Simon glanced at his watch. There was still time to make it to Vegas, still time to explore these feelings he had for Emma. So what if she was a distraction? He was due a distraction or two. Emma, with her Christmas-green eyes, sparkling spirit and moral indignation was just the kind of diversion Simon needed.

He opened the door and went to help complete these last deliveries.

"HOW DID WE END UP with this small delivery?" Simon asked. Despite her suggestion he sit this one out, he stood at the rear of the car looking at two small bags of food and gifts Emma was pulling from the trunk.

"I always deliver to Mrs. Brennaman," Emma said. She glanced up at the sky. If it would only snow, it might help her forget that his tender kisses led nowhere. "I think everyone in town had her for kindergarten, but she always told me I was her favorite."

"Merry Christmas," Simon said defiantly when Mrs. B. opened her door.

Emma echoed his sentiment, her smile forced.

"Come in, dearies," Mrs. B. said, peering

at Simon through her thick glasses. "You look very familiar to me, boy."

"I'm Simon Castle."

"Of course you are. You must have helped Emma with deliveries last Christmas. Come in, come in." She shuffled to one side of the door so that they could enter her cluttered living room.

Newspapers and magazines were stacked on the floor by the couch, which was draped in a half-finished afghan. Framed photos of Mrs. B. and her husband at various ages crowded the coffee tables. Simon picked one up for a closer look.

"That's my husband." She took the picture from Simon and stroked the frame with her thumb. "People live such fast lives nowadays. Not like Bill and I used to. That man. He loved to surprise me. One night when we were hiking the Sierras, he made me a bed on sugar pine branches. It was like sleeping in a tree."

"You can't get that in a hotel." Simon's voice was gruff.

"No, you can't." Mrs. B. beamed at him. "I know you're in a hurry tonight, so I won't keep you. I'm always grateful for the Santa Express. Make sure you thank everyone for me."

"We'll stay as long as you like." Simon reached for Mrs. B.'s hand.

How could Simon come across as cold one minute, yet charm the socks off Emma and Mrs. Brennaman the next?

"You've stayed long enough already." Mrs. B. patted his hand.

Emma deposited a small bag of gifts on the couch and gave Mrs. B. a careful hug. "I'll come and get you on New Year's Eve. Momma wouldn't want you to miss her party."

"Thank you, honey." Mrs. B. turned to Simon, who stood silently taking in the cluttered apartment, which couldn't have been as big as one of his hotel rooms. "I bet in kindergarten you used to pull someone's pigtails." Mrs. B. gestured for Simon to come closer, and then she said in an audible whisper, "If you had gone to school here, I bet you would have been my favorite student that year."

When Emma gasped, Mrs. B. turned to her. "Honey, you know I tell every former student they were my favorite. I'm so fond of all of you I could never choose just one."

Simon winked at Mrs. B. and laughed, the sound falling over Emma like so many

Christmas morning snowflakes, with a hypnotic quality that was impossible to ignore.

"Now, skedaddle. I know you have more deliveries." Mrs. B. shooed them out.

As soon as the door closed behind them, Emma wrapped her arms around Simon's neck and kissed him. She'd be content to be snowed in with this man.

And then Simon was kissing her back, sharing his warmth, pulling her so close she wished their clothes would disintegrate, removing all barriers between them. His hands—those heated, magical hands!—traced their way beneath her jacket and up the curve of her spine before delving back the other way.

"Ooooh."

Emma wasn't sure who moaned. She'd take credit if he asked—as long as he didn't stop kissing her long enough to ask.

A door opened. "Who's out there?" Mrs. B. tapped on Emma's arm. "It's Christmas Eve. Don't you two have someplace else to go?"

Laughing, the pair ran hand in hand to the car as snowflakes started to fall.

When Emma reached in her pocket for

the remote, Simon stopped her. "Wait. I haven't kissed a girl in the snow in a long time."

Emma tilted her head for his kiss, accepting his need, disclosing her own.

Someone drove by and honked, sending Emma into a fit of giggles.

"I'm sorry. I'm so sorry. I'm attacking you and it's Christmas and we've just met." She gazed up into Simon's dark eyes, unable to keep from smiling because she wasn't sorry in the least.

"You know me well enough," he said gruffly, and she realized it was true. "Anytime you want to give me another present—" He tugged her hips against his. "Anytime you want to kiss again under the mistletoe, you just let me know."

"It's a long way to Las Vegas," Emma said, already wondering if he'd invite her to stay a few days after he attended that all-so-important meeting, wondering what she'd say if he did, wondering if what she felt for him was love or infatuation. She voted for love. "I'll have to ask you to sit in the backseat."

He buried his head beneath the hair at her neck and nibbled on her skin. "I won't be in that backseat alone again." With his clever hands playing across her skin, she couldn't even articulate an answer.

Another car drove by, reminding Emma that they needed to get on the road as well. There were three more deliveries and many miles to travel. Reluctantly, Emma backed away from Simon when all she wanted to do was burrow beneath his overcoat and cling tightly to this wonderful man.

EMMA ROBERTS WAS JUST WHAT the doctor ordered for his annual Christmas blues. The holidays were going to be different this year. Hell, the new year was going to start with a bang—successful business ventures and the promise of something that had been missing from Simon's life for far too long.

"Just one more delivery," Emma said, turning down a court lined with rusted, sometimes lopsided mobile homes.

Simon's fingers were linked through hers. One more delivery and they'd be on their way to Vegas. He hadn't expected the deliveries to be so difficult, so joyous.

In companionable silence, they unloaded a box of food and the bulky present Doc had wrapped and carried them to the door.

"This is Johnny's friend, Wallace," Emma said when a small boy opened the door. Wallace stuck out his hand for a manly handshake.

"Johnny told me you'd come," Wallace said.

Simon hesitated a moment when he realized Wallace only had two fingers and a thumb. But he recovered quickly and shook the boy's hand firmly, uncomfortably aware that while his own smile had wavered, Wallace's never had.

"It's all right," Wallace's mother softly reassured Simon.

"Can I open my present, Mommy?" Wallace asked. "Johnny told me to wait up and I was really good all day, just like you asked." He put both hands up to his cheeks and Simon saw that his left hand only had two fingers and a thumb as well.

How on earth was that boy going to play the piano? There must have been a mistake. Simon tried to catch Emma's eye, but she was watching Wallace.

"It's all right with us," Emma said, smiling as if Wallace had the brightest future ahead of him.

Wallace sat down in front of the big

package on the floor and tore off the wrapping paper. For a moment, the boy sat frozen, staring at the box and Simon was sure there had indeed been a mistake.

And then Wallace jumped up and down, ran to each adult in the room and hugged them, shouting, "I asked and I asked and I got it!"

Simon found himself grinning and hugging the little dynamo back.

"Can you get it out of the box for me?" he asked Simon.

"Of course." His throat nearly closed with emotion, Simon's voice sounded gruff. He carefully opened the box and set the keyboard on the kitchen table, plugging it into the wall outlet.

"He plays at school, but hasn't had anything to practice on," Wallace's mother told them, wiping tears from her eyes. "I knew it was a big gift, but I hoped..."

Emma hugged her and pressed something into her hand.

As Wallace plunked his fingers on random keys on the keyboard, his mother unfolded two hundred-dollar bills. She began to cry and hugged Emma again.

Where had Emma gotten two hundred

dollars? But Simon knew. He couldn't decide if he was proud of her or angry with her for giving some of her money away. Despite all the advice he'd given her, Emma didn't care about her own future. Simon reached for her, intent on pulling her aside when Wallace struck the first few notes of Beethoven's Fifth Symphony, his face aglow. Simon's jaw must have dropped halfway to the floor. The kid could play better than most people with ten fingers.

"When you first came in, I thought you were someone else." Wallace's mother gave Simon a hug, then drew back with a sad smile. "I used to work as a maid at the Castle Hotel in Reno, but Mr. Castle would never do anything like this."

Simon stiffened, but the woman didn't seem to notice. She only had eyes for Wallace now.

"Mr. Castle put in these lovely new featherbeds that are supposed to be heavenly to sleep on. But they were also heavier to make and it took longer to change the sheets," she explained. "I couldn't make my quota and Mr. Castle didn't care. So I lost my job and came back here to live with my dad."

The reality of her situation hit Simon with a knee-knocking force that almost brought him down. Simon retreated toward the door, letting Emma return their wishes for a merry Christmas as she followed him out. He pulled the hated Santa cap off his head and started to get into the front seat, then thought better of it and tossed the hat there. He climbed into the backseat and retrieved his BlackBerry from his pocket but didn't look at it. "Let's get to Vegas."

CHAPTER NINE

"You LIED TO ME." Emma jammed the key into the ignition, then froze, cold for the first time that evening.

She could have fallen in love with him.

It took her a few moments to work up the courage to turn and confront Simon. "That's why the rat is in your parking lot, isn't it? Because it's harder for the maids to keep up now that you've changed the bedding and the union knows it." *Please, please deny it.*

"That's right." He sat in the corner of the backseat, his face in shadow.

"Nothing lasts forever, Simon. Did you know that?" Emma faced forward, blinking rapidly. She'd let desire cloud her judgment. Simon was just another heartless guy who put himself first. She bit her lip. "When you're gone, do you know what will happen to Castle Hotels? They'll be sold and demolished. That's the way it is in Nevada. No one will remember you."

"It's all right, Emma."

"No, it's not. Do you know why men like Carnegie and Rockefeller live on in history and have monuments dedicated to them?" She drew in a ragged breath, trying not to let him know she was breaking apart inside. "Because they *gave back* to the community."

When he didn't fight for her—or himself—she dug into her pocket and threw the remaining bills over the seat. "Here's thirteen hundred dollars. The keys are in the ignition. Drive yourself to Vegas."

"We had a deal." Simon didn't want to go without Emma, which was ridiculous. All she'd done since she'd met him was make him doubt himself and his goals. He caught one of the bills before it drifted to the floorboard.

Without a word, Emma opened her car door.

"You're not like me, Emma." Of course, not. She had a conscience. "You'll regret that you didn't uphold your end of the bargain, either tonight as I drive away with your car, or Tuesday when I ask my lawyer about breach of contract." He might still have the power to keep her with him, at least for tonight. "Think of all that money you'll owe me if you don't."

"It always comes back to money." Emma clutched the wheel, bowing her head.

Simon wanted to pull her into his arms and tell her everything would be all right, but he knew that was a lie. Mrs. B. would continue to spend her holidays alone. Wallace would grow bitter as he realized how handicapped he was. Even little Johnny would find that life wasn't as easily won as a wrapping contest. Simon had made a choice long ago to be the kind of man Emma would never be able to love because that's the kind of man who got ahead in the world.

"I didn't ask for your sympathy about the rat. At the time, I didn't think it was any of your business." Simon's stomach churned. He really was a selfish, heartless bastard. It was best she knew it. "I stand by my decisions. All I ever asked was for you to drive me to Las Vegas." Why wasn't she arguing? Before Simon knew what he was doing, he reached for her. Just in time, he drew back, staring at his fingers as if they'd betrayed him.

He needed something to do with his hands. A punch of a button illuminated his BlackBerry screen and one new message.

Assuming your plane is delayed. Please confirm your attendance upon arrival in Las Vegas. Erik Wiseman.

Steven Wynn wasn't soft. George Maloof wasn't soft. Simon Castle couldn't afford to be soft. And neither could Emma. Anger drowned out his sorrow and pity. "Thirteen hundred dollars? Didn't Marlene give you twenty-five hundred? Did you give two hundred dollars to every family?"

"Yes." Emma closed the door and started the car, shifting gears before the engine fully caught. The Town Car lurched away from the curb with a groan.

"Twelve hundred dollars?"

"Yes." She hadn't missed the hardness in his voice because Emma's had developed something just as edgy.

Good. If nothing else, perhaps this interlude would teach her to be more selfish with herself and her dreams. "We visited six homes. If Doc and Owen hadn't caught up with us, would you have given away another twelve hundred?"

"Yes." Just the way she said it made him

believe she saw absolutely nothing wrong with giving away a good chunk of the five thousand dollars he'd promised her.

"You'll never be anything more than a chauffeur, Emma." Simon sank into the seat. "You have to think of yourself first."

"Like when you offered to stay longer with Mrs. B.? Or when you helped Wallace set up his keyboard?" Emma gave him a quick glance in the mirror, but it was too dark to read her expression. "Your trouble is that you don't want to care about anyone but yourself."

"No." If he hadn't cared for the people he'd met tonight, it wouldn't hurt this much. "But I can't help everyone and myself at the same time."

"Everyone? What about a few?" Emma drove through the center of town, past the businesses that had been refurbished into their original Old West charm. "You helped six families tonight, six very special families. You helped a woman who lost her job because of a decision you made."

"And that's supposed to make me feel better?" Emma couldn't possibly under-stand what he was going through. Simon wanted to be the kind of man Emma deserved, but that man couldn't also earn enough money to buy back his father's love.

Blood roared in his ears, drowning out all coherent thought but the truth.

"Emma, stop the car." He was going to throw up.

"What?"

"Stop the car," he yelled, not waiting until she had completely stopped before getting out.

On unsteady feet, Simon staggered across the asphalt to the icy sidewalk. He stared inside the dark windows of an Old West saloon, wishing it were open so he could down a shot of whiskey and try to ease this frustrating pain. All this time, he'd thought—

"What's wrong?" Emma slid on the ice in front of him, holding on to his arms so she wouldn't fall.

Simon couldn't speak. Not now. Not when he was seeing his mistakes clearly. He stepped back, desperately wanting perspective and for his stomach to stop churning. He could have been happy with one hotel, but he'd called his dad and listened when he'd said Simon's success wouldn't last. "Give me the keys."

Emma looked confused but didn't resist when he pried the keys from her fingers. "What about—"

"Go home, Emma, before I change my mind." Simon had to do this alone. He wouldn't ruin her, too. "You can walk home from here. I'll make sure your car gets returned to you."

"But—"

"Go!"

He couldn't watch her leave him, but he did listen to the soft tread of her feet on the thin layer of ice as he clutched one of her hundred-dollar bills.

Simon didn't know how long he stood there waiting for something—lightning to strike, a ghost to tell him he'd been a fool. Nothing. His nose began to run from the cold. All the money in the world wouldn't bring Simon's mother back. His dad would never love him. He'd lost Emma, probably lost career opportunities in Vegas, and would most likely suffer a severe setback from the inflatable rat choking in garland in his parking lot.

The question was—what was he going to do about it?

Simon curled his hands into fists, squeezing the remote control so hard the car alarm went off, startling his feet right out from under him.

"IS THAT YOU, EM?" Donna Roberts called as Emma let herself in the front door. "Did you complete all your deliveries?"

"Yes." Emma wiped away tears with icy fingers. "Mrs. B. says hello and thank you."

"Did Wallace like his keyboard?" Emma's mom peeked around the corner of the foyer, wearing her red-and-green terry robe. "What's wrong? Where's Mr. Castle?"

"Trying to get to Vegas." *Without me.* Emma should be counting her blessings that she wasn't with him. She swept an afghan from a living-room chair over her shoulders.

"Emma Noelle Roberts, did you leave him alongside the road on Christmas Eve?"

Emma let Momma believe Simon was stranded. "He wants to turn Virginia City into a little Reno, complete with a hotel, twenty-four-hour restaurant and casino."

Momma started to say something, then stopped to consider this latest development. She straightened her robe. "The jobs would be welcome."

"Momma, he's heartless."

"That's not true." Her chin had a stubborn tilt to it. "I saw him wrapping presents this evening. He reorganized everything and he helped you load up the car."

"Only because he knew I wouldn't leave until after the Santa Express deliveries. The most important thing to Simon Castle is his bank account. All he thinks about is how to improve it."

Momma crossed her arms. "Really? Then why did he leave his briefcase here?"

KARMA REALLY SUCKED.

Stars flashed in front of Simon's eyes. Something terrible had happened and Simon was helpless to stop it. Everything was quiet and cold.

Gradually, he became aware that he was clutching something in each hand. Curious, he unfurled his fingers to find a set of car keys and a one-hundred-dollar bill. A soft breeze sent the money tumbling out of his grasp. Money didn't matter. Emma was right. People mattered. Like his mother, whom he'd never really allowed himself to grieve for. And Wallace with his stodgy determination to follow his heart instead of the logic those around him tried to force on him. And Marlene, who handled every curve he threw her way, in a wheelchair, no less. And Emma, good-natured, eternally optimistic Emma.

Four calling birds, three French hens, two turtle doves...

Now he was imagining things. He heard angels singing.

And a partridge in a pear tree! The song died away. How fitting that he was hearing the last lines when he was at the end of his rope.

"Look! Is that a man on the ground?"

Simon was feeling more like the money-grubber that Emma had accused him of being than a man at the moment.

Footsteps rushed toward him. Shadowy Victorian figures surrounded him. Simon was either dreaming or dead and about to be trampled by the ghosts of previous Virginia City residents. It was nothing less than he deserved.

"I'm a doctor. Are you all right?" A face with fogged glasses swam in front of Simon. Fingers probed the back of his head.

"Ow!" Simon's eyes widened as the man found a tender spot at the base of his skull.

He became aware of his back, cold against the icy sidewalk.

"Can you wriggle your toes? Move your fingers?"

"Yes." His digits felt like ice cubes.

A spotty-faced teenage boy leaned into Simon's line of vision, a top hat on his head. "Is this your money? You shouldn't walk around with so much cash." He waved Emma's one-hundred-dollar bill in front of Simon's face.

Earlier today, Simon would have bet he'd never see that cash again.

The group surrounded Simon in their velvet coats, top hats, Victorian dresses and shawls, bringing him unsteadily to his feet.

"You're lucky David spotted you as our choir was making a last pass through town. Otherwise…" The doctor gave him a serious look. "Well, it's Christmas. We'd best not talk about what might have been. Do you know someone who can drive you to the hospital? You should get an X-ray."

"I'm going to be fine. I don't have time for that." With a firm handshake, Simon pressed the bill into the other man's hand. "Donate this to someone in need, will you?"

The doctor searched Simon's gaze before

looking down at the bill and then holding it up for the rest of the choir to see.

There were cheerful calls of "Merry Christmas."

Convinced he'd done the right thing, Simon no longer felt cold. This feeling of well-being had to be what kept Emma warm in her tuxedo shirt. Maybe there was hope for Simon yet.

"Can we give you a lift somewhere?" the doctor asked.

"My car's right there." Simon pointed at Emma's Town Car.

"Are you sure you want to drive? You've got quite a bump there."

"I think I've suffered worse injuries." Simon paused. "But thanks for asking."

"MERRY CHRISTMAS." SIMON pushed open the door and stepped inside, nodding to Emma and her mother. His overcoat was missing and he had a bad case of Santa-hat hair that was endearing.

Not that Emma cared. She wrapped the afghan tighter about her shoulders. "What are you doing here?" Whatever he was after, Emma wasn't in a giving mood. Giving in to Simon meant getting hurt.

"I couldn't leave town without apologizing. I—"

"I won't accept." Emma cut him off and turned away.

"Emma," her mother admonished. "Your manners."

"It's all right, Mrs. Roberts. Emma and I understand each other." Simon looked at Emma in a way that made her want to forget what a butt head he was and remember how tenderly he'd kissed her. But that was what had gotten her into trouble in the first place.

"Oh, yes. You forgot your briefcase." Emma took a step toward the hall.

"Did I?" He reached for Emma's hand, his eyes so intent upon her that she stopped. "I've harbored lots of dreams for all the wrong reasons, Em. And now I have just one Christmas wish."

Simon gently tugged her closer. "I've got a lot to make right in Reno. Come with me. Tonight. I know it's Christmas, but that's the best time to make amends." His voice dropped. "Say yes. Give me a chance to prove I'm more than the heartless suit who manipulated you into driving him to Vegas on Christmas Eve."

Emma could barely fill her lungs with air.

"What about your meeting? Your hot prospect for success?"

"I e-mailed them my regrets. There are more important people to be with on Christmas." Simon's smile was hopeful. "Besides, I'm pretty happy with the prospect in front of me."

Emma didn't dare hope, and yet… "Why should I say yes?"

"Because there's something between us and if I go to Vegas I know I'll lose it. I'll lose you, Emma."

Momma gasped and sank against the wall, whispering, "I've never heard anything so romantic. If you don't say yes, I just might."

Emma laughed, finally letting herself believe that the man she'd caught glimpses of throughout the night really did exist. "It's not a proposal, Momma. That won't come until later…when he's proved himself." To both himself and Emma. "Yes, Simon Castle, I'll go with you to Reno, if only to make sure you know how to give properly."

Simon's kiss was far too brief. They had too much to do.

EPILOGUE

"I NEVER KNEW MAKING these beds was so difficult," Simon admitted, tucking the sheets tight around the corner of the king-size bed and all its special padding, wishing he could crawl into it with Emma and not get out for days. "Do you think I should get rid of them?"

"Nope. There are standards to be upheld at Castle Hotels," Emma said, picking up the large goose-down comforter and heaving it into the middle of the mattress. "You do want repeat business, after all."

"I think next year I'll hire more staff and offer those bonuses in advance of Christmas." Not first thing Christmas morning like this year. Simon had been lucky to get some of the staff to come in.

"We're done with our side of the floor," Mrs. Roberts said, sticking her head into the room. Her smile wasn't as bright as it had been the night before.

"This is the last room on our side." Emma smoothed out the comforter and began plumping up pillows.

Owen and Doc appeared behind her, looking as worn out as Simon felt. Many of the Santa Express workers had driven up to Reno after midnight when their deliveries were done. Simon checked his watch. Between the regular staff and Simon's volunteers, they'd managed to clean all the rooms by noon.

Owen arched his back. "I'd say Christmas dinner—"

"And the beer," Doc was quick to add, although his grin was frayed around the edges.

"—are on you, Castle."

There was a whir in the hallway and Marlene appeared in her wheelchair. "The presidential suite is ready for your guests, Mr. Castle."

"Thank you. Can you escort these gentlemen and Mrs. Roberts to the suite?" Simon looked at Doc, Owen and Mrs. Roberts in turn. "I hope you don't mind sharing the presidential suite. It's the best in the house. We'll have dinner brought up in less than an hour."

"I knew you were a good man the moment I laid eyes on you," Mrs. Roberts said when she was done hugging Simon.

"You turned out all right," Owen allowed as he shook Simon's hand.

"Oh, I almost forgot," Marlene said. "The rat is gone."

"Owen, you didn't…" Emma gave her brother a suspicious look. He'd mentioned something about doing away with the rodent when Emma had explained why it was there.

"I'm too tired to shoot the rat." Owen frowned.

"Don't worry. I called the union rep and told them about the changes." Simon turned his attention to his secretary—the woman he'd been with longer than any other.

"Marlene, did you get in touch with Frank, Richard and Carrie?" He'd instructed Marlene to give his overworked driver, hotel manager and assistant the next two weeks off, as well as notify them of their Christmas bonus. As soon as things were under control here, he'd let Marlene start her two weeks. He'd also called Wallace's mom this morning and promised her a job if she still wanted to work for him.

"I did, sir."

"Please, call me Simon." He met Marlene's gaze squarely, aware of Emma's hand on his shoulder. They'd talked about this on the drive back to Reno. "I was wondering if you wanted to move into my rooms here at the hotel. I'm going to need a bit more privacy now." He glanced back at Emma with a smile. "Everything here is wheelchair friendly, you know, and the staff would be at your command."

Marlene looked flustered. She'd weathered so much with Simon that he could understand her being unwilling to trust him.

"She may want her space, Simon," Emma said softly beside him, trying to give Marlene an out.

"If she does, I'll just have to arrange for her to move. She deserves a better place to live." He'd had Emma drive them by Marlene's place on the way into town. He couldn't imagine a woman in a wheelchair feeling safe in that neighborhood. "Just so we're clear, Marlene, I'm reducing your hours, not increasing them. Although I am giving you a promotion to vice president of operations with a generous raise because I can't get along without you."

"Yes." Marlene released a breath, eyes bright. "Yes, sir…Simon." She put out her hand to shake his, but he leaned closer and hugged her instead. When he straightened, Marlene handed him something. "Your BlackBerry."

"Not on Christmas, Marlene." Simon didn't even glance at the screen. He only had eyes for Emma.

When Marlene had led the others to the elevators, Simon locked the room he and Emma had cleaned. She leaned against the wall across from him, her expression so warm Simon couldn't imagine he'd ever be cold again.

"Thank you," he said.

"For what?"

"For somehow seeing something that no one else—not even me—could see. I'm not sure I'll be able to live up to your expectations." He'd known this amazing woman less than a day, yet he was scared he'd make a mistake and ruin everything.

Emma closed the distance between them, a mischievous shine to her eyes. "Simon, let's make a New Year's resolution to fall in love…and to love each other until there's no Christmas spirit left in this world."

"No Christmas spirit left in the world?" He laughed, opening his arms for her. "That won't happen in our lifetime."

"Exactly."

Dear Reader,

What fun it was to write this book. An expectant mom on a luxurious train, speeding through the snow toward a family Christmas in a cozy Virginia City home. A good man, intent on claiming the woman he still loves—and the child he didn't know about. I loved telling this story.

Of course, I had all the answers. Rachel Ford and Andrew Durham don't even understand the truth about their past as they embark on the Santa Superchief. They can't see a future.

During a night filled with Christmas carols and labor pain—and visitors who remind Andrew and Rachel how fragile family is—they begin to see visions of what could be, if they reach out to each other and dare to believe in the future they want.

Because believing, at Christmas, makes dreams come true.

I'd love to hear what you think. You can reach me at anna@annaadams.net.

Best wishes,

Anna

ALL THE CHRISTMASES TO COME

Anna Adams

First, to the girls on the third floor of Hawkes—Sarah's other family: Cresta, Julia, Margalena, Riley, Erin, Laura, Meredith, Nicole and Ali. While we've been far away, she's had love and a home with you. How can I ever thank you?

And to Brenda and Melinda—thanks for letting me spend this Christmas with you. I loved brainstorming, chatting, writing—and especially getting to read your stories first. Working with you has been a holiday!

CHAPTER ONE

DEEP IN RESEARCHING contract law for a legal textbook he was writing, Andrew Durham only realized he wasn't alone when the door to his home office slammed into the bookshelves behind it.

"Andrew, get your ass out of that chair. Rachel's having your baby, and she moved out of her apartment today. Find her or you're going to regret this moment for the rest of your life."

With all the grace of someone who'd been hit over the head with a plank, Andrew spun his chair to face his sister. Temper radiated from Delia's eyebrows to her pink-tipped nails.

"What?" After *Rachel...your baby* he'd lost the thread. "That can't be right. Rachel?"

Having *their* baby?

Delia rushed at him. "Get up. Do something. You two took months to decide you were wrong for each other. You don't have months now." She yanked his arm so hard he fell off the chair. His teeth rattled when he hit the floor, but the bump to his butt cleared his head.

"That's why she left." Last Christmas he'd proposed—over tinsel and evergreen and Bing Crosby crooning her favorite holiday songs. He'd set the scene after they'd put his daughter, Addie, to bed. He'd balanced on one knee, feeling idiotic but hopeful. Only to watch Rachel back away from the green velvet box that held his grandmother's ring—which he'd saved for the perfect woman.

The perfect woman had asked him how he felt about having another child—their own. Shocked because he'd never kept his feelings secret, he'd explained again that he couldn't start over with all that new-father stuff. He'd met Addie's mother at a conference. Neither of them had mistaken a weekend for a relationship. Nine months later, as unprepared for parenthood as he, she'd literally dumped Addie on his doorstep.

Savage, protective love for his daughter had bowled him over. He'd learned to be a dad despite no god-given paternal instincts. And had abandoned a promising law career to write legal texts from home.

Last Christmas Addie had been five years old. He'd finally begun to breathe again. Starting over with car seats and diapers and vaccines and sleepless nights... Worrying that a simple cold would advance to pneumonia because he didn't know what to do next?

Not even Rachel could convince him that sharing the work and worry as well as the good parts would make it all better and easier.

Enduring an uneasy truce, they'd tried to make things right for a few months, but Rachel wanted what she wanted, and he wouldn't even pretend to be the man to give it to her. They'd loved Addie too much to continue the tension and escalating arguments. Rachel had packed her things and left. At the time, her sudden departure had stunned him. Now he got it. Her pregnancy—with his child—had made escape urgent.

"How'd you find out, Delia?"

"You broke up with her. I didn't. She was my friend, and I stopped by her place to give her a Christmas present. Her apartment's empty, and her car's gone. The landlord said she shipped the car and she's taking some train home to Virginia City." Delia reached to help him up.

"It's called the Santa Superchief. She rode it every holiday with her parents when she was a child." Andrew stood by himself, leaning toward the window over his desk. His office faced the backyard. Addie and her friend Joey came running from the side of the house, peppering each other with the Wiffle balls he used to practice his golf swing.

Christmas in San Diego wasn't exactly snowsuit-and-mitten time. Virginia City would be a lot colder. Would Addie's coat even fit?

"Will you make lunch for the kids?" He started for the door. "And I don't mean order pizza, Delia. We can't wait for that."

"Now is not the time to make fun of my cooking. Where are you going?"

"To find warmer clothes for my daughter." He turned back and yanked his middle desk drawer open, digging inside. "I have Mrs. Ford's phone number somewhere.

Rachel's probably planning to stay with her mother."

"The landlord said she's gone for good, you damn idiot."

"Remember not to swear in front of Addie." He hated sounding like a tight ass. Maybe Rachel had thought he was one. She'd left him, left their home without saying a word about a baby.

Delia pushed him toward the door. "I'll find the number. Why'd she go now? The landlord said she'd be lucky to get over the state line before she delivered."

"I guess she was desperate." He couldn't meet his own sister's eyes. "Or maybe it was because the Santa train was a tradition in her family." They'd planned to take Addie as soon as she was old enough to enjoy the two-day trip.

"You should call for a reservation." Delia sounded calmer, her way of trying to comfort him. "Do they let you reserve seats on a train?"

"The best seats on this one go early. I'd be lucky to get Addie and me on it at all."

"You have to try. Forget about calling Rachel's mother. She'll tell Rachel you're coming, and your baby could disappear."

"I thought you were still Rachel's friend."

"I am." Delia's frustration tightened her voice.

"Then what are you saying? She'd never try to hide the baby from me now that I know."

Delia pushed her hands down the skirt of her dress. "She *has* run away. She left you in May, and she had to have known she was pregnant."

After he'd insisted for months he didn't want another child. "You know how we argued. She believed I wouldn't want the baby—I kept saying I didn't want to start over with more children."

Delia made a *come on* face, but suddenly clenched her fist. "Why didn't I think of this before? Call Rachel. You must still have her cell-phone number?"

"She changed it." After she'd asked him to stop calling. He nodded toward the yard again. "Will you call the kids in?"

"Sure."

He phoned the train line. They still had a couple of coach seats. They'd sold out the compartments months ago. He made two reservations.

Then he grabbed jeans and sweaters for

Addie and himself and shoved it all into one large zippered push-bag. He couldn't find Addie's winter coat so he snatched up a pink sweater and a white sweatshirt. She'd fit into the holiday landscape like a plump, pink snow-girl.

Downstairs, Addie and Joey were choking down black-crusted grilled-cheese sandwiches and tomato soup under Delia's fierce prompting. As he came into the kitchen, Addie shoved her bowl away, streaking the counter with red soup.

"What's wrong, Daddy? Aunt Delia's being scary."

"I'm sorry, honey." Delia wiped Addie's chin and then tugged her close. "You have a surprise. Daddy's been getting your things ready."

"Joey, I'm sorry we have to send you home." Andrew interrupted Delia to keep her from saying anything that might raise Addie's hopes about Rachel. The mother of his unborn child might ask him to jump off the train the second she saw them, and Addie'd already mourned her for months. She didn't need any more disappointment.

Delia nodded. "Maybe this little one should stay with me."

He hesitated and faced a truth he'd rather avoid. He didn't want to hurt his daughter, but he'd use her if Rachel gave him no other choice. Rachel had decided he didn't love her, but she'd have a hard time turning her back on Addie twice. He needed time to convince her he'd been trying to protect her, not reject her. Besides, Christmas Eve was only two days away. "I don't want to be away from Addie at Christmas no matter what happens."

"Oh. Yeah." Delia reached for the little boy. "If you're ready, Joey, I'll walk you home."

"Sure. Mom's making cookies." He poked at the burned edge of his sandwich. "She gives them away to the people she works with, but I just beg till she lets me have a couple."

Andrew patted the boy's shoulder. "Excellent plan. Merry Christmas, son. Addie, are you ready? You can finish your sandwich in the car."

She and Joey exchanged a look, and she grabbed a coloring book and crayons from the dresser behind the table. "Let's go."

"Andrew, I have that phone number." Delia passed him a scrunched-up sheet of paper. "I wonder if you should make it all fair and call?"

He glanced at his watch. Playing fair would be foolish. Besides, the train left in an hour. "Thanks, but we should go. If traffic's bad…" He couldn't miss that train. If he had to race it to each station, he would.

Delia caught him in a quick hug. "I'm so angry with you for—" She stopped. "But I'm so afraid you're going to lose your chance with this one."

"Me, too, and this time it's all my fault. Come on, Addie." He grabbed at his daughter's hand, and she ran to catch up.

"Daddy, what's wrong?" Her uncertain blue eyes melted his heart. "I think you're mad."

"No, bunny." He drew her to his side, smoothing her pale brown hair. "It's like Aunt Delia said. We're leaving for a Christmas surprise, and I don't want to be late."

"Will I like it?"

He tried never to lie to her. "I hope you'll love it, baby, but sometimes you can't be sure until the surprise works out." She'd have a lot to deal with—a new brother or a sister. She already loved Rachel like the only mother she'd ever had.

Why hadn't it been this easy to see another child in their lives last Christmas? A little boy—another girl maybe—who nuzzled her bottle and sucked her thumb with Addie's contentment. He didn't think Addie'd suffered a lot, stuck with him as a single dad, but he was starting to feel helpless again.

How could he make Rachel understand? He'd been foolish, but now that he knew about the baby, he wanted it as much as he wanted Addie. It was Christmas. He could use a miracle that made Rachel believe.

CHAPTER TWO

"LAST CALL FOR the Santa Superchief. All aboard—and kiddies, look sharp—we never know if a jolly old elf will hitch a ride."

The conductor's patter hadn't changed in all these years. Rachel Ford eyed the gray-haired man in his ornate blue uniform. Was he the same guy?

Watching him over her shoulder, she kept moving. If she stopped, she might need the assistance of a crane. Thirty-eight weeks pregnant, she moved with the litheness of a beached whale. She pulled her bag, counting down cars. Perspiration gathered beneath her bangs.

In front of her, a man and woman pulled their luggage while a girl of maybe three danced on tiptoe between them. In a red coat too warm for San Diego, she peered into the train windows to catch Santa lurking.

Rachel slid her free hand across her belly, far too heavy with child to feel so hollow. She'd meant to be on the train early, but she'd had a lot of goodbyes to say.

She'd even driven past Andrew's house one last time, angry with herself, still pining for him and Addie. He hadn't loved her. He'd made up that ridiculous story to get rid of her. What kind of a man—a good father—expected a woman to believe he doubted his ability to be a good father twice?

But why would he lie to her after he'd asked her to marry him? It never added up. Only leaving had made sense.

Addie and Joey hadn't seen her, too engrossed in strafing each other with Wiffle balls. On the verge of giving birth to Addie's baby sister, she'd turned the rental car around and driven to the rail station.

Struggling down the red carpet lined with oversize faux peppermint canes, she tried to soak up some of the happiness around her. She reached her car at last and started climbing the steps, but a conductor grabbed her bag.

"Let me get that for you," said the woman.

"It's heavy," Rachel said, as the handle left her fingers.

"All the more reason. Let me see your ticket." She needed only a swift glance. "Ahh, compartment A. Good—you'll have your own restroom."

Rachel laughed, having paid dearly for that privilege. It already felt like money well-spent. "You've been this pregnant?"

"Twice." The woman held out her hand. "Call me Maggie—and promise you won't go into labor on my train."

Rachel crossed her heart. "If I have anything to say about it." She was heading home to her own mother, who loved her unconditionally—although she insisted Rachel was wrong to hide Andrew's child from him.

Maggie wrestled the bag up the last metal step. A few feet down a narrow, wood-paneled corridor, she opened a compartment door. "Here's your home for the next two days."

Rachel took in plush burgundy velvet and more of the strangely luminous paneling inlaid with pale carved flowers. "Wow— this is more luxurious than my apartment."

"Mine, too," said Maggie. "Now, you're

probably wondering about dinner arrangements."

"My first concern."

In the warmth of Maggie's good humor, Rachel found her lost sense of anticipation. Her doctor had argued against moving, but had finally faxed Rachel's records to her doctor in Virginia City with the disgruntled hope that she wouldn't have the baby before she or the records arrived.

The train's outer doors clanged shut, and she jumped. The engine powered up and the train rocked once. Rachel leaned down, desperate for a last glimpse of San Diego. She'd made the right decision, so why did she feel afraid? Guilty, even.

"We won't be moving for a few minutes yet." Maggie peered through the window. "Are you looking for someone? Anybody joining you?"

She shook her head. Her hair brushed her face, and the tickling sensation dragged her back to the real world. Andrew couldn't have been clearer about not wanting children with her.

"I'm moving home, but I've lived here for about seven years, and I'm going to miss the city." The city... Be honest. She ached for the man she still loved—and his daughter— who might have been hers, too, if Andrew hadn't been so afraid of the future. Without him and Addie, staying had become pointless.

No matter how hard she'd tried not to think of them, her life and theirs remained entwined. She rubbed her stomach again. The baby stretched, no doubt wondering where all the space had gone.

As if she sensed Rachel's unspoken heartbreak, Maggie squeezed her arm. "Can I get you anything?"

"No." Rachel turned away, sniffing hard. "Thanks, though."

"The dining car is two down. Turn left out of your door." Maggie crossed the small space and pointed at an ivory-colored button with a glowing red dot in the middle. "This calls me any time. Whatever you need." As Rachel lifted her eyebrows, Maggie grinned. "You've heard that old saw about bartenders being good listeners? They have nothing on train conductors."

"Anything to keep me out of labor?" Rachel asked.

"Well, yeah." Maggie opened the door. "You unpack and I'll come back when dinner's served. You sure I can't bring some herbal tea? Maybe a pack of crackers?"

"I'm way past morning sickness." She leaned against the door as Maggie went into the hall. "I'm not normally such a weakling."

"I'm not normally so understanding and helpful." Maggie went to the next compartment and pressed her finger to her lips. "Don't tell your neighbors."

Grinning, Rachel shut her own door. Her smile faded as she faced herself in the gilded mirror.

"HEY," ANDREW SHOUTED at the conductor who was gripping the train's last open door.

"You're almost too late," the other man said, but he came down the stairs already reaching to help with the bag. He glanced at Andrew's tickets. "Come aboard here. They've shut the doors up ahead. You're just a few cars on, but you can reach it through the corridor." He yanked their bag up the stairs, freeing Andrew to lift Addie. "Have you heard who's traveling with us this trip, miss?"

"Who?" Addie's gaze was almost too serious. "My daddy says this is a Christmas surprise. Are those real peppermint sticks back there?"

"Not those." The conductor eased the door shut behind Andrew. "But someone you're going to like will bring you treats later. I'll put your things away for you, sir. Later, at bedtime, you can get any belongings you need."

"Thanks."

Andrew set Addie down and turned her in front of him just as the train jerked forward and kept rolling.

"We're going, Daddy."

What if Rachel hadn't made it? How comfortable could a train be for a woman so late in pregnancy? He measured all the moments he'd lost, the days and nights his child had been growing inside her.

He'd had a right to know, but he rubbed his mouth and tried not to feel angry. It wouldn't get him anywhere. Right now, he had to find Rachel.

Addie scuffed her sneaker toe on the plush carpet. "Daddy, this is nice. I thought the train would be all metal like in the movies."

The walls were paneled in wood more expensive than any surface in their house.

No wonder even the coach seats had cost so much. "Hold my hand." He steadied her as they entered a new car, but Addie tumbled against an older man's shoulder, and Andrew eased her back, preparing an apology. The man's warm smile startled Andrew.

"Merry Christmas, little girl," he said, clearly more in the grip of the season than Andrew felt.

"Thank you, sir. Same to you."

"What a polite girl. You must be excited about this trip?"

Addie frowned. "Well, I wanna know about the surprise." She swung around to Andrew. "Who's coming, Daddy? Someone I know?"

The man and his wife laughed, but a palpable longing made them serious. "They're that young for so short a time," the man said.

Andrew understood the man's regret. The past six years spun past his memory, the happiness of Addie's unrestrained joy in any colorful toy that caught her fancy, frightening illnesses that worsened with terrifying swiftness in childhood, the first time he'd had to leave her with a babysitter.

Doing it all alone, he'd been grateful to survive—continually surprised to find Addie thriving. Maybe he should have managed to live a little more—and appreciate.

How had he fallen into the same situation with another child? He'd been careful with Rachel. So careful he'd driven her away. He obviously had more to regret than the couple gazing with nostalgia on his little girl.

"Merry Christmas," Andrew said and led Addie through another car to their seats.

She scrambled on her knees across burgundy velvet to claim the window. "I like this train." She pounded the fat, luxuriant upholstery. Carolers entered the car from the other end and she sang along in their homage to Rudolph. She hung over the back of the seat until the singers left, and Andrew managed to pull her down beside him. "We're going faster and faster."

And time was speeding past, too. "Are you hungry?" The dining car might be a good place to search for a pregnant woman.

"Remember Aunt Delia gave me that yummy sandwich." She rolled her eyes. "I'm starving."

"Aunt Delia tries." He craned his neck for a conductor. "Wonder when they start serving dinner?"

"Where are we sleeping?" Addie kicked her legs up and down. "Does this turn into a bed?"

"No, but it reclines."

"Huh?"

He showed her. "You think you'll be able to sleep here tonight?"

She hated change and loved her own little bed. "Are you going to make me wear my jammies in front of all these people?" She skewered the young couple across from them with a resentful look.

"No." He hadn't thought this out. He could end up ruining Christmas for his daughter, as well as losing her younger sibling. "We'll just brush our teeth. They'll have blankets." Even airlines still offered blankets.

"Sounds strange." She returned to her window. "I usually sleep in a bed, and I have all my toys. Can I get my baby out of the suitcase?"

"Sure."

"Good, because she doesn't like being in the dark too long." She sat finally and turned to the window.

Andrew took her hand between his. She smiled at him, but her eyes looked wet. "This will be fun, Addie."

"Okay, Daddy, but you'll stay awake?" She sandwiched his hand between hers, barely covering his palm. Then she leaned against him. "I don't know anyone else here."

"I'll take care of you. You'll always be safe with me." He hugged her until she squirmed away.

Addie had been his first concern for six years and now he was risking her peace of mind. He had no choice. If things worked out, Addie would have a sister or brother and her beloved Rachel back, and that was a future worth risking.

CHAPTER THREE

"I CAN BRING YOU A TRAY," Maggie said.

Her offer tempted Rachel. The seat hugged her body, and she felt all warm and cozy. But her doctor had cautioned her to get up and walk often during the trip. "Thanks, but I've got a thing for Santa."

Maggie held the door. "He's started his rounds so you have a shot if you've been good this year."

"Pretty good." She hadn't intended to be bad. Her birth control had gone awry and she'd lied by omission. Of course, Addie niggled at her conscience. Rachel and Andrew had made their own choices—but that meant Addie would never know she had a little sister.

Rachel balanced against a cool, wide window in the hall. "It's getting colder already."

"We're starting into the mountains."

Maggie glanced back as they reached the next car door. "That your first baby?"

"Yeah." She'd considered Addie her first for a long while. You only had to watch Addie for a second with other children or with the dolls she loved and nurtured to know she'd be the best big sister in the world.

"Here we are." Maggie opened the dining car door.

Again, the walls glowed, their warmth reflected in crystal and gleaming silver. Rachel eased into a place set with bone china. It should have been fun, a break from her normal life. This year, the holiday train was simply a way home. Kind of a waste, when she spied the happy families around her. "Thanks, Maggie," she said.

"While you're eating a good meal for that baby, I'll make your bed. It's a little early, but you could probably use a few extra hours' rest."

Maggie turned away, and Rachel peered at her own face again, this time in the mercifully blurry window. Grief could make a woman look haggard, and she was mourning Andrew and Addie as if she'd left them today, not seven months ago. She'd secretly hoped Andrew would come after her and be delighted with the baby.

Fool.

The door at the other end of the car opened and a little girl skipped through, her light brown hair swinging in a ponytail. Rachel's breath caught. She looked like... Her grief must be stronger than even she guessed.

"Addie."

She'd wanted to see her, been tempted to climb out of her car and hug the daylights out of her, but was she hallucinating? Beaming, Addie hopped to a table, the small, happy spirit of what this Christmas should have been.

"Wait, sweetie. The waiter will seat us."

That voice. It had whispered love words in her ear and broken her heart.

Andrew and Addie. She wasn't hallucinating.

Andrew was thinner, his face drawn. He caught Addie before she could climb into a chair at the empty table she'd appropriated.

Rachel only realized she was trying to stand when her stomach hit the lip of her table. Addie and Andrew were real. Not spirits. Not what should have been. They'd come.

To find her?

As if the tide of Rachel's hope swept into Addie, she turned. Rachel's whole body clenched at Addie's joy.

"Rachel!" She ran, slipping this way and that, until she fell into Rachel's arms. Her hug was as tight as a noose, but then she hopped backward.

"What's wrong with you?"

Rachel nearly choked on a laugh. She couldn't make herself look up at Andrew so she focused on his daughter's wide eyes.

"I'm—" Would Addie understand? Would Andrew want her to know? "I gained some—"

"Rachel's having a baby," Andrew said.

Rachel read nothing but bleakness in his dark gaze. He'd given up hope. He had to know the baby was his.

"Are you angry?" She forgot Addie for a moment.

"Yeah," he said, "and shocked."

"How can you have a baby, Rachel? You don't have a daddy for it."

"The same way I have you," Andrew said. "Except she does have a daddy. I'm the daddy for Rachel's baby."

"How? Don't daddies live with their babies?"

"I hope so."

"Not always." Rachel tried again to stand, but Andrew touched her shoulder.

"Please."

His hoarse voice cut straight to the bone. He'd blurted out all the things she wouldn't have dared tell Addie.

He had lied to her last Christmas. He obviously wanted their child.

But her plan hadn't included him. He'd turned his back on her and the family she'd wanted—more than she'd wanted him.

"I can't do this." She gripped the table ledge, creasing the rough tablecloth. "Maybe we can talk later, but right now—" She looked down at her belly, at the baby that would be here before she learned how to handle Andrew.

"Later is too late." His gaze followed hers. "We aren't going to reason with each other. You're carrying my child."

"I don't get it," Addie said. "Are you and Daddy married, Rachel?"

"You know daddies and mommies aren't always married." Andrew's desperate expression admitted this was more complicated than he'd expected.

"Daddy and I are friends." Friends—the last thing she'd ever wanted to call Andrew.

"But I'm going to have a brother."

"Actually, you're having a sister," Rachel said.

"You know?" Normally, the man in control, Andrew sounded as if he couldn't get enough air.

She empathized, reaching for her water glass as the world spun. "Yes."

"Daddy, Rachel and my sister need to come home with us."

"I agree."

"No," Rachel said again.

"I'm asking you to—"

"I know what you're asking." Marriage. In front of Addie? "You didn't want me or—" She stopped. Some things, Addie didn't need to know. She touched her stomach and avoided the pain in Andrew's eyes. She'd hurt him. That much was clear. "It's too late. I don't want you this way."

"No." Andrew lifted Addie into a seat across from Rachel and then took the chair beside her. "It's just in time."

"I have to live with my sister." Addie leaned across the table to take Rachel's hand.

Rachel closed her fingers around Addie's.

"Don't worry. You'll always get to see your sister." How, when Addie lived in San Diego, and Rachel planned to stay near her mother in Virginia City?

"I'm the big sister. I have to take care of the new baby." She looked to her father to back her up. "Right, Daddy?"

"Absolutely right." He didn't touch Rachel, but she felt tension in his knees against hers, in his mouth, too tight to ever smile again.

She felt his need for their baby, who was never supposed to be his. "How did you find out?"

"Your landlord told Delia and she told me."

"I should have asked him not to say anything."

"Thank God he sang like a canary."

"That's not funny. I didn't want you to know. In fact, you made it clear you didn't want to know."

"I was wrong. You can see I love Addie more than anything."

More than he'd ever loved the mother of his new child. That was all she needed to know. A woman wanted to be somewhere in her husband's priorities. She wasn't jealous of Addie, but she wanted Andrew to love her as much as his little girl. She deserved that much. "I'm not in trouble," she said. "I want a family, not resignation from a man who finds himself with a familiar problem."

"Neither—" He also stopped, aware of what he shouldn't say in front of his daughter. "No one around here is a problem." Addie straightened, opening her mouth slightly. Andrew turned to see what had snagged her attention, but then leaned toward Rachel. Daring to take cover behind Santa's entrance. "Every argument I made looks foolish now, and I'd take it all back. I want you and the baby. *I* want our family as much as you do."

"Words are easy." She took advantage of Addie's fascination with the man in red, too. "I never believed you—it was too ridiculous." He straightened with wounded eyes, heartrendingly like Addie. "You'd never have tried to see me again if I weren't pregnant."

"Because I didn't want to hurt you," he said. "You wanted a life I didn't think I could give you. The baby changes everything."

"You can be a good father without marrying—"

"Daddy, he's here. Turn around. He's got candy in his pockets."

Rachel fought her own body's awkwardness, trying to stand as Andrew turned to Santa. She finally found her feet, intent on getting out of there even if she had to wrestle Santa for wiggle room.

"Wait." Andrew grabbed her arm. "I'm asking you to marry me."

"I noticed," she said, as her way out narrowed even more. "You don't want to be caught in a custody fight."

"I have rights." He didn't even try to pretend she mattered.

"Nice." She let bitterness into her tone. "Don't threaten me."

"What?" As if he didn't understand.

"You aren't taking my child and you'd better believe I'll never walk away." Without volition, her glance slid toward Addie, whose mother had done just that.

Andrew let her go and she felt chilled—because of his coldness. "You know me better than that," he said.

"You made up a crazy story to get rid of me."

"I asked you to marry me. How can that mean I didn't want you?"

"How could you not be a good father the second time around? You're great with Addie."

"I must be better than I thought if you can't see how scared I am that I'm screwing her up." He lowered his voice, as Addie glanced back, but she was only checking to see if they'd noticed Santa. "I'm sorry, Rachel. I was wrong. I even brought Addie and told her about the baby. That must show you I'm serious."

"Only if you're trying to convince me you'd use one of your children to blackmail the mother of another."

As soon as Santa made room, she eased past him—and he plugged the hole between Andrew and the aisle as he handed Addie a candy cane.

CHAPTER FOUR

THE DOCTOR HAD TOLD HER to walk the aisles. A few hours later, Rachel followed his prescription—just to keep her circulation active.

She also searched each face in the coach section, but she'd never admit she was looking for Addie and Andrew. It was too late to trust his change of heart. He harbored no secret love for her. He wanted his child, exactly as he wanted Addie.

In the fourth compartment behind hers, she found them. She grasped a seat back, watching Addie twist for comfort, a frown lining the soft skin between her closed eyes. She rolled toward Andrew, her hair standing on end as she lifted her head.

"I can't sleep, Da—" She saw Rachel. "There you are." She dove over the edge of her seat. Andrew looked up, too startled to stop her. Addie reemerged, brandishing a jewel-toned candy cane. "Santa gave me this for you, Rachel."

"Thank you." She had to go closer, to take the candy. "Did you ask for an extra?"

"Yes, because you like candy canes."

"I'll sure keep this one." She held it with both hands, close to her heart.

"You have to eat it before it 'spires."

"What are you doing here, Rachel?"

Not much of a welcome in Andrew's abruptness.

"Rachel?" he said again.

"I don't know."

He leaned toward her.

She clutched the candy cane even closer. And she latched on to the one excuse Andrew wouldn't question. "Addie," she said. "I wondered if Addie was sleeping well."

"How did you know where we were?"

She'd hoped to see them. If they'd been in a compartment, she'd have wandered—searched—the length of the train and gone back to her own bed. "You couldn't have bought your tickets as early as I did."

"I'm very tired, Rachel, and I can't sleep." Addie gave her father a stern look. "I need a bed."

"I have one." And she must be out of her mind, subjecting herself to the grief of saying goodbye to Addie again. Because she'd have to. "There are two in my compartment. Like bunk beds. Could you sleep on a top bunk, Addie?"

"Can I, Daddy?" Addie was dangling off the end of her seat again. She rose with a well-loved doll, one with brown matted hair and painted brown eyes, half kissed off her face.

"I recognize her." She'd given the doll to Addie last Christmas.

"This is Rachel." Addie held her up with pride, like any mother. "Rachel, meet Rachel. You can kiss her," Addie said.

Rachel kissed her namesake because otherwise she would have had to swallow a lump the size of Mount Everest and find words. The doll hadn't shared her name before she'd left Andrew and Addie.

"Are you sure about sharing your room with Addie?" Andrew asked. "I don't want you tiring yourself, and my girl is a Chatty Cathy at bedtime."

"Specially in a strange bed." Addie had clearly heard about her failing before.

Andrew ruffled her hair. "Have you been

standing on your head? Your hair's starting to look like your dolly's."

"Can I go?" She started clambering over him and he grabbed at her as her hands and feet dug into him.

"Wait," he said. "We have to talk."

"We'll talk in the morning." Why dither? She had a chance to spend unexpected time with Addie, and those minutes were growing shorter as the train rushed toward Virginia City. "Day after tomorrow, you're going back to San Diego. I'd like to share the compartment with her."

He knew this was her last goodbye. His face went blank. His usual defense when emotion threatened. For a second, she wondered...

Not for long.

"Let's get your things, Addie. Have you brushed your teeth?"

Her enthusiastic nod should have rattled the teeth right out of her head. Rachel took Addie's hands and helped her the rest of the way over her father.

"Kiss Daddy good night, and we'll put your Rachel to bed."

Addie wrapped an arm around her father's neck. He kissed her, but he never looked away from Rachel. He had a right to be confused. She couldn't explain her own behavior because she couldn't forget days and nights filled with wondering what they were doing, how much Addie had grown, whether Andrew thought of her once in a while, too.

The baby kicked suddenly as if reminding her she had more serious problems now.

"Meet me for breakfast," Andrew said.

"What time, Daddy?"

He turned his watch over and grimaced. "It's almost three in the morning. Let's say around ten."

"Will they still be serving breakfast at ten?" Rachel asked, not trying to evade him. "I wouldn't want Addie to miss eating."

"I'll probably be awake and I'll come get you if they're going to stop earlier."

Letting awkward seconds pass, Rachel nodded and turned Addie toward her own compartment. Maggie was in the hall.

"Would you mind lowering the other bed?" Rachel asked. "I'm having company."

"Sure." She smiled at Addie with the wistfulness of a mom who missed her own children and then made up the other bunk as if she'd been dying to work in the middle of the night. Rachel thanked her, and Addie echoed her, sounding sleepier by the second.

"I'll probably stay awake," the little girl said after Maggie shut their compartment door.

"Probably." Rachel helped her into bed and gave the other Rachel's slightly dirty face another swift kiss. She tucked Addie's blanket up to her chin. "Sleep well, sweetie."

"I can't." Her eyes were already closing. "You'll be here in the morning?"

"Absolutely." She wished she could promise to be there all the mornings of Addie and Andrew's lives. She cradled her big belly in her own arms. She couldn't promise anyone what the future held.

She'd never understood how leaving could hurt so much when leaving had been the only answer. Familiar loneliness bore down on her again, at higher speeds than the train was going.

A MAN WITH ANY SELF-RESPECT wouldn't show up half an hour before he was due to meet a woman, but Andrew couldn't afford self-respect. How could he explain how much he'd missed Rachel, how he'd refused to let himself think of her because the smallest memories of her—always a little windblown, always laughing—had made him want to crawl to her?

Talk about a jackass. He still loved the woman whose love he'd killed. Lurking outside the dining car, he kept glancing at his watch. His situation was too dire for a trick, too important to trust mere honesty to save him. Rachel seemed to believe only their unborn child had brought him to this train.

"Daddy, Rachel's room is better than our chairs."

Thank God. Addie was dragging Rachel toward him. Rachel, who rocked from side to side with the movement of the train and her unaccustomed girth.

"Did you sleep well?" He took her hand. He could pretend he wanted to steady her, but he needed the touch of her skin.

"I'm fine," she said.

"Won't you let me help you?"

Her steady gaze was answer enough.

"Help me, Daddy. Hold me up so I can see what's on that table. I'm starving."

He lifted Addie so she could see the buffet of fruit and bagels and croissants. She stretched. "I don't see eggs."

"Maybe you can ask for them." Rachel's love-rich voice shortened Andrew's breath.

He studied her face, which was thinner, more delicately honed by impending motherhood. Her smile for Addie revealed her weakness. She might despise him, but her feelings for his daughter had only deepened.

Their turn came to be seated. Addie hovered over her chair. "Can I go look at the food, Daddy?"

He could use a moment with Rachel. "Don't touch anything."

"I'll put my hands behind my back."

Rachel laughed. That had been their answer to Addie's compulsion to touch every object she came near. Since birth, his tactile daughter had been fascinated with textures, which often caused trouble in bakeries or clothing stores they visited after a bakery.

"Should you let her go that far away by herself?"

"I'd reach her if she needed me."

Rachel faced him. "I know that about you."

"But you don't think I'd do the same for you."

"You want to help. You want your child

now that it's real and not a nebulous possibility."

"I was wrong, Rachel." He cut to the chase. "I still get terrified every time Addie has the sniffles, and I'd rather be vaccinated myself than see her go through it. I don't find diaper changing cute and car seats are an enigma wrapped in a mystery, but I'll do it all again. I want to do it all again. With you and this child." He reached for her, but she turned away.

Her skin flushed.

He gripped the table to keep from slamming his fist onto it. "You don't want me to touch you. Your first instinct is to keep my child away from me."

"I know I can't do that." She turned to make sure Addie was out of earshot. Still she lowered her voice. "Now that you know, I won't oppose visitation. I want Addie to know her sister."

Her troubled gaze searched his face. At last, he saw a hint of doubt. He waited, afraid to ask if she was thinking of giving him a second chance—if she could still want a family with him.

"I haven't changed. I want a husband who adores me *and* cherishes our child."

"What if that's me?" he asked.

She considered, but then she spurned him with a shake of her head. "If you loved me, you'd say so. You wouldn't ask if I thought you could."

CHAPTER FIVE

"ARE YOU MAD AT DADDY?"

"No, honey." Rachel tried to settle Addie and her doll in bed that night, but Addie wriggled to a sitting position, baby Rachel clutched in an over-affectionate hug.

"Why wouldn't he let me come see you all day?"

"You're here now." And Rachel had to wonder if Andrew had deliberately kept Addie with him to leave her alone with traitorous thoughts.

"Because I made too much noise for the man in the seat across from Daddy. He kept staring at me, looking mean until Daddy said I could sleep here again."

He'd dropped her off and said good night, questions in his eyes, rejection in the stern set of his shoulders.

"I'm glad we get another sleepover." Letting Addie go after this would be fresh torture. No woman should have to give up an almost-daughter twice. She should hate Andrew for that alone.

"You like my daddy?"

Sort of. Not often. "Sure I like him." Rachel forced a smile that felt more like rictus. "Now you and little Rachel get some sleep. Do you want me to read you a story?"

"And sing me a song. I like Christmas songs right now."

"We'll try some more Rudolph."

It took the exploits of Rudolph, Frosty and the mean Mr. Grinch before Addie nodded off with a bit of baby Rachel's hair in her mouth. Rachel considered pulling it out, but decided against possibly waking her roomie.

A knock at the door startled her. She snatched it open, not altogether stunned to find Andrew on the other side. He glanced over her shoulder. "Is Addie awake?"

"She just fell asleep."

When he looked at her with widened eyes, she remembered Addie had been playing with her hair while she sang.

"You had to wrestle her into her bunk?" he asked.

She tilted her head, trying not to smile,

pretending he only irritated her. Without Addie as their buffer, she was more aware of him. The spice that scented his skin, his still unfaded tan from taking Addie to their community pool. Those crinkly lines beside his eyes had seduced her more than once.

She pulled back. No more seduction.

"Wait." Andrew caught her wrist.

She wanted to resent his touch. Instead, she imagined him sliding his hands down her back, pulling her into the heat of his body.

And she grew weak. Take advantage of a man's guilt just to appease loneliness that had stalked her with memories of him? Not a chance.

"Good night, Andrew."

"Come out here. Talk to me."

She shook her head. "We've said everything."

"Let's talk about the future."

With one hand on her stomach, she reached for the door handle. "I know my future."

His mouth opened. She almost felt the breath easing between his slightly parted lips.

His pain should have pleased her. She'd

wanted him to hurt as she did. She'd thought she wanted to hurt him.

"I'm sorry." For what? "I mean I don't want you to feel bad, but think how bad we'll both feel if we get married and then you find the woman you want to share your life with."

"You are that woman." But he'd told her too many times that he didn't want the children—the family—she yearned for.

"I'm smarter than you," she said, "about this anyway. You kept saying you couldn't be with me because I wanted children and Addie was enough for you."

He pulled the door shut, in case Addie should hear.

"What you meant was, you didn't want those things with me. You love family. You're going to find the woman who makes you want more."

"We have a family." He pulled her close, actually smiling as her belly bumped him. "You and I were raising Addie. Believe me when I tell you I was an ass, and I pushed you away when I should have been on my knees, begging you to stay."

"Make me believe you." He looked blank, and she shook her head, shrugging at the same time. "That's the problem. You can't, and I can't stop believing all you want is this baby."

The baby seemed to be lulled by train travel. After a relatively quiet day and a half, she stretched—or something that made Rachel's stomach tighten as if she'd stumbled into a python—and then the protest kicks started scrambling her organs.

It was like carrying a goalie who was practicing for a big game. She supported her stomach with both hands. Andrew looked down.

"What?"

"Hard kicks." Focused on her body, she managed a grin. "Trying to find more room to stretch, I guess."

"Are you sure you're all right?"

"I have about two more weeks." The baby settled back down. "Maybe I should have waited, but I've gone through this whole thing alone. I was even afraid to tell my mother at first."

"She must love me."

"More than me, I'd say." Her ears still rang with the constant admonitions. "From the moment I told her, she said you had a right to know."

"You should have listened."

His voice was low and husky. She had to be using up his store of restraint, but he'd left her no choices.

"I thought this baby was going to be mine alone." She inhaled, so aware of Addie, asleep in her compartment. "This may be the worst time to discuss what you want, but I'd just as soon have it out of the way."

"I want my child."

Not the woman carrying his baby. Just his child. "That goes without saying." Paranoia gripped her. "But you'll have to deal with a mother this time."

"Rachel, do I have to tell you you're hurting me? Do you know how many times, in the middle of the night, I wonder how Addie's managed to survive? If you think doing it alone makes it easier, you have a rude shock coming."

"The past nine months have been filled with rude shocks."

"All nothing compared to what comes next."

Andrew's parents had divorced when he was two. His mother had tried to be a good parent, but she still seemed perpetually bewildered by the turn her life had taken. His father had "graduated" from most of the rehab clinics on the California coast. Andrew had hardly seen him since Addie's birth because he didn't trust the man, and he didn't want his daughter picking up any bad habits.

"I don't know how much nurturing we learn from our parents." Her mother was equipped with lioness instincts. "But Addie is strong and happy. I hope our child is as healthy and well-adjusted. Especially now."

Down the corridor, the door opened and Santa weaved toward them. He held out his hand to Rachel. She'd grown used to strangers being affectionate with a mom-to-be so she shook his hand.

"Your little girl made quite a bargain for that extra candy cane."

"Did she?"

"I love kids like her. She told me not to bother bringing her minioven because you might believe in me if I gave you the candy." He laughed with Santa-gusto. "She reminded me what Christmas is supposed to be. That's why I take this job."

"Does your family mind spending Christmas on the train?" Surely he didn't leave them home over the holiday.

"My wife left me several years ago," he

said, sobering. "The kids are all grown. I get back a little Christmas every year on this train." He looked past them. "Maggie, girl, I have stockings for your two."

Maggie, who'd appeared out of nowhere, went with Santa after a careful glance at Rachel.

Andrew came close enough for her to feel his heat in the cooling space. "Why do you hope especially now that the baby will be well-adjusted?"

"She'll be living part-time with you and part-time with me." She'd rather her daughter—and Addie—had a conventional, Mom-and-Dad family.

"We have to talk about you living in Virginia City," Andrew said.

And so it started. But she recognized the bravado behind his arrogance, so she tried to be gentle. "That decision's made. I want to live near my mother."

The baby stretched again. She caught her breath and flexed one hand against her compartment door. Outside flashed a landscape of time-honed mountain and flying snow.

"What? Rachel, what's wrong?" Andrew looked her up and down as he would a firework that might go off without warning.

"This kid must be stretching from head to toe." Andrew's anxiety was contagious. "But I'm not going to explode." She touched his shoulder. Pressing her palm against his hard muscle felt strange and yet painfully familiar. "The baby's fine."

He moved and her hand hung in midair until she flattened it on her stomach, as if she didn't feel rejected.

Andrew fiddled with the drape that half covered the window. "You don't believe I could want you back?" Anger seeped into his eyes and curled his fingers. "Even though I never wanted you to leave?"

"I don't come to your mind first. You're here because of this baby."

Turning from the window, he faced her again. "I thought I wasn't right for you. I've had luck with Addie. I wouldn't have tempted fate again, but if you could have settled for me and my daughter I never would have let you leave."

"It wouldn't have been settling."

She was lying and they both knew she'd wanted her own babies that badly. She looked away first, feigning interest in the frozen night. Though every inch of the train exemplified luxury, a hint of must drifted off the curtains. "Pregnancy plays up your sense of—" Again, her stomach tightened, but this time, pain radiated from the small of her back. "Oh, God."

"Rachel?" He caught the fist she tried to press into the base of her spine. "Are you—"

"I'm wondering. It hurts." It really hurt—a cramp in her back and then something more than tightness across her stomach. A contraction. "It might be one of that false kind."

"False kind?" He held on as if he could save her with his strength.

"You know—Braxton-something."

After a moment, he smiled—probably despite himself. "You know less than I do. Braxton-Hicks, Rachel. You didn't read a book?"

"Several, but I can't remember everything when I'm about to give birth on a train." She grinned, a little queasy. "You know they'll charge me extra for leaving with a new passenger."

"You make it worse when you try to joke. So do me a favor and don't until we know you're safe." He maneuvered her toward her door. "Let me get you inside and then find a doctor."

"No." She pulled his hand off the doorknob as he tried to open it. "Addie."

"Addie will have to adapt," he said.

"Find the doctor first. Let her sleep a little longer."

He wanted to argue. She saw it in the vein that had risen at his temple. Instead, he let her go, and she could have sworn he said something under his breath as he turned away.

"Wait."

He stopped. "I need to get you help."

She hated being beholden to him of all people. "There's a button near the bed with a red light. If you press it, the conductor will come. But don't wake Addie."

"If I do, I'll tell her I came to say good night."

"Okay." The threat of another—whatever it was—persuaded her. "But try not to wake her."

"Sure." How could he make that one word imply she'd lost her mind?

He slipped inside and a second later came out again. A few minutes passed like several hours with Andrew watching her.

Maggie returned, surprise arching her eyebrows. She realized right away what was going on. "Rachel, you promised."

"We could be wrong. Neither of us is very experienced."

Maggie nudged Andrew with a smile. "You and I may have plenty of time to discuss that, considering your little girl. For now, I happen to know we have a doctor two cars down. He'll be so excited when I put him to work."

She made her way down the train, leaving calm behind her.

"He'll check you out and tell me to get off your back and let you sleep," Andrew said.

As a new pain started, Rachel tried to keep a straight face—and prayed Andrew was right.

CHAPTER SIX

"WE MIGHT AS WELL WAKE that little girl of yours," said the man who'd introduced himself as Dr. Tinsley. "She may be learning a lot about life tonight." He checked Rachel's pulse. "I can't tell where we are without an exam, but this young woman looks like most others I've seen who are about to deliver a baby."

"Don't say that," Rachel said.

"I've heard women stop being rational in labor."

"Andrew, you may think saying that in a dry tone makes it less insulting. It's not."

"We can stand in the hall and count contractions half the night, or I can carry Addie out here and let Dr. Tinsley find out what's going on with you. But only one of those options is sane."

Dr. Tinsley folded his arms. "My wife will come looking for me if I stay for contraction counting, and she doesn't like having her Christmas interrupted."

Another pain gripped Rachel. "I'm not afraid of any mere woman. Aliens," she said, rubbing her taut belly, "now they scare me."

"You're not carrying an alien. You're just afraid. What's your name again?"

Andrew actually groaned. The doctor looked at him, light from the fixture above his head glinting in his sliver hair. "I'm bad with names, but great at delivering babies. I'll give you a list of satisfied clients."

"Sorry." Andrew took the situation into his own hands and opened the door. "Addie, time to wake up a little, sweetie."

Rachel held on to the doorjamb. In a moment, Andrew returned, his daughter lolling in his arms. "I'll wait right here," he whispered.

And it mattered. Now that the moment presented itself, she didn't want to deliver alone. "I'm supposed to be tough," she said. "Women on this very ground delivered their babies and then skinned a rabbit if they were lucky enough to find one."

Andrew paled. "Skinned a rabbit?" He tucked Addie's head beneath his chin. "Are you okay?" He turned to Dr. Tinsley. "What's happening to her?"

"You're both overreacting." He nodded at Addie, still asleep. "You're having another baby, not a national emergency. Come along before your daughter wakes up, and then we're all in trouble."

Her mouth was so dry her tongue no longer fit. Rachel drank in the sight of Addie, her soft face even more delicate against Andrew's sweater. "Whether I wanted to share the birth of our child with you or not, we're in it together now."

He dared to look relieved.

"Now changes nothing," she said. "When this train reaches Virginia City, I'm putting—" She lowered her harsh whisper because she didn't want Addie to hear or think she didn't still long to live with her. "I'm putting you on a plane to San Diego."

THE SECONDS TRUDGED like centuries as Andrew rocked Addie with the motion of the train. At last Rachel's compartment door opened and Dr. Tinsley looked a touch more serious.

"She is in labor," he said. "Why don't we take your daughter to my wife? We're on this train to take her mind off the fact that our grandchildren are in Paris for Christmas. She'd welcome your little—"

Please God, let him be better at his job than he was at remembering names. "Addie," Andrew said, "and don't take this badly, but I don't know you or your wife. I'm a little reluctant to hand my daughter over to—"

"I've never had to try so hard to do anyone a favor." Dr. Tinsley wrapped his stethoscope around his neck with enough annoyance to make himself wince. "I have to tell the conductor what's going on, and I'll ask her to move my wife as close to this car as she can."

"Thanks. It's not as if I don't feel like an idiot." He pressed his chin to Addie's head. "But she's my daughter."

Tinsley's face softened. "Come with me. The sooner we get back, the sooner you can join your wife. She's going to want your company soon."

"Soon?" Andrew turned down the hall, unable to avoid looking back at Rachel's closed door. He ought to tell the doctor how things really stood, but they'd already given the man enough trouble.

"She's only had a few contractions, but she's dilating quickly. Let's find the conductor and my wife."

After they explained to Mrs. Tinsley, she looked at Andrew as if he were Santa bearing the gift of a child she could care for. Maggie moved the doctor's wife and Addie into the seats closest to Rachel's compartment. With Addie settled, complaining in her sleep, Andrew returned to Rachel. Tinsley and Maggie were discussing what they'd need.

Andrew knocked on the door, breathing hard.

"Come in."

His hands were sweating. He rubbed his palms together and opened the door.

"You're back." Perspiration beading on her forehead, Rachel rose from her slump on the seat. She caught his hands, and the fear in her grip dissipated his. He pulled her close.

"Shouldn't we stop this thing and get you to the nearest hospital?" He breathed her scent off the top of her head. He'd missed her so much that even now, holding her almost made him forget....

"Dr. Tinsley says it's probably quicker to

get to Virginia City. There's not much between here and there." She wrapped her arms around Andrew's waist. "I *am* okay, and he doesn't mind giving up his last night on the train to help me. I trust him even if he is a little bossy." Linking her hands behind his nape, she pulled herself close again.

He leaned over her, realizing she was having another contraction. "Funny how you trust that guy right away."

"I kind of have to."

"Are you positive? You're comfortable with him, Rachel?"

"I've forgotten what comfortable feels like."

"Another one already? Maybe you should sit down?"

"Dr. Tinsley said it was going to happen fast. I'm not sure I'm ready to be a mom. You don't think I caused this, leaving so late in my pregnancy?"

"Maybe seeing me caused it." He hugged her. It took this to make them talk as they had before, like friends, lovers, about-to-be parents. "Babies come when they're ready. We'll be ready, too. I learned to be ready for Addie."

"She's going to make the best big sister." Rachel pulled away, but when she looked at him, he couldn't read her feelings. "When you all visit the new baby."

He let it go. "Why don't you sit down? Try to relax."

Another knock at the door preceded Maggie and Dr. Tinsley. The other woman planted her hands on her hips.

"So I really can't trust you." Maggie eased Rachel to one side. "Let me open your bed. Do you want some ice chips? The doctor tells me that's all you can have. Nothing else to drink or eat."

"I'm fine."

"You all step outside so I have room to work, and we'll be all set."

"I'm just going to have another word with my wife," Dr. Tinsley said. "She didn't plan on a working Christmas."

Andrew watched him hurry along the thick carpet. "She won't mind. She all but thanked me for letting her watch Addie. Have you noticed how many people are on this train because they miss their families?"

"It was always like that. There were always older people traveling without children, but I never noticed it before."

"I guess it's one way to celebrate Christmas with children around." He might never be sure he was the best father Addie could have, but he sure counted on every Christmas with her. He dreaded the day she claimed her independence, even though a healthy childhood would train her to do that.

Rachel held the door, her fingers trembling against the heavily lacquered wood.

"Try not to be afraid," he said. "I'll be with you."

She stared hard, but he didn't want her to read his unsettled mind. At last, she relented. "It hurts already, and I have a feeling it'll get worse before it's better."

"If I could do it for you, I would."

She tried to hide a smile. She had the right to laugh.

"I'm not trying to be smarmy. I let you down, and I wish I could make it up." Words stuck in his throat. "You can believe in me."

"I have to now."

Her tart humor seduced him. She braced herself in the doorway and endured another contraction with her eyes slitted and her body hunched.

He wanted to twist the train like the toy it resembled. Something. He had to do something. Helplessness made him turn away. Being afraid now felt sensible.

"You don't have to have a plan for every contingency." Her voice came through gritted teeth. "Neither of us expected this."

"The baby?"

She straightened with tears starting in her eyes. He'd never seen Rachel cry because of pain. Once, when she'd come upon a guy hitting his dog in the park, she'd boiled over with rage and she hadn't even noticed she was crying. She'd all but demanded the guy hand his dog over to her as she'd love it instead of trying to beat it into submission.

"I know you didn't get pregnant on purpose. I thought you might have meant going into labor on the train." Where had that doctor gone?

"I jumped to conclusions." Rachel grabbed her stomach. "I think the baby has decided to break out the hard way."

"Any way at all looks hard to me."

Rachel's mouth opened slightly. Her moist lips caused him an untimely jolt of desire. He tried to hide it, but she laughed and he wanted more than anything to hold her.

Behind her, the door opened and Maggie ushered them in. God, for an ambulance.

"Do you want to change clothes?" Maggie asked Rachel.

Andrew cursed himself for not thinking of it.

"I have a nightshirt," Rachel said.

"Put it on, then. I have a list of things to collect for Dr. Tinsley."

Andrew left the small compartment on Maggie's heels.

"Andrew," Rachel said, her voice tight with pain. "Don't go."

He froze. All these months without her and now she wanted him to help her change?

She coughed, but he saw the fear she was trying to conceal. "I don't want to be alone."

"Okay."

"Keep your back turned, though. I don't want you to see me this way."

"You've never understood the first thing about me." As if he wouldn't find her body, swollen from carrying his child, attractive.

"I believe you now, about being afraid. It doesn't change our situation, but I believe it could make you do crazy things." A sudden sound he didn't recognize nevertheless punctuated her declaration cum warning. "Oh, God. My water just broke."

He had to help her.

"No." A zipper opened and more rustling mingled with Rachel's soft groan. He tensed, but she must have noticed his involuntary movement. "Don't, Andrew."

"I can't let you suffer."

"It'll be worth it in a few hours. I won't have any dignity left, but maybe I won't care once I hold my baby."

He turned then, in time to see the well-worn, blue-striped, white nightshirt drift over her swollen belly, her slender thighs, her cold-looking knees. His throat locked. If she believed he'd been terrified of starting over, he had a chance to convince her he'd been an idiot and knew better now. "*Our* baby."

"Take on your half of what I'm feeling now, and I'll be impressed."

She eased onto the bed, her face as pale as the sheet beneath her.

"Let me get that damn doctor back here."

CHAPTER SEVEN

"AM I GOING TO DIE?" Only half joking, Rachel grabbed Dr. Tinsley's arm. With the grin of a man who'd heard it all before, he removed her clawlike grip and patted her shoulder.

"You may wish you would, but no. In about an hour or so, you're going to give birth. What a way to start Christmas Eve, huh?"

She tried to agree. Over his shoulder, she saw Andrew, ashen-faced, also trying to smile. No matter how glad she was to have him with her in this torture chamber, telling him so would have made her too vulnerable. "Don't you dare faint," she said, when what she meant was "Don't leave me. I'm scared."

He flexed his hands, and only then did she realize what an iron grasp he'd taken on her small sink. "I'm fine," he said. "Until you start screaming again."

Offering the doctor even a veiled apology was easier than letting Andrew know how much she needed him. "I guess I was counting on that epidural."

"I can't believe your regular physician advised you to take this trip," Dr. Tinsley said.

She was in the mood to blame someone else, but honesty prevailed. "He argued."

"A sometimes pointless exercise with heavily pregnant mothers."

"Like you, he was a touch patronizing, and he couldn't understand how much I needed to be with my own mom."

She inhaled. *Breathe through the pain.* Ridiculous concept. But it took concentration and maybe stopped women from going for the throat of any male within reach.

Dr. Tinsley grinned and rolled down his sleeves. "Won't be long now. Let me check with Maggie on a few things." He clasped Andrew's shoulder as he passed. "And I'll look in on your little girl, too." He shot Rachel one more look. "Try to focus on the reward of holding your baby."

"Thanks," Andrew said.

She hated him for a moment. He lowered himself to the side of her bed. "I was right, you know," he said, his irony a clear attempt to comfort her. "Watching you in labor is the most horrific thing I've ever seen. When does all the beautiful stuff start?"

She laughed as much as she was able. "Weakling. You should try it from this side."

"I'd rather." He stood and strode two steps that took him to the window. "I hate having no control."

Which explained why he'd been so afraid of having another child. A lifetime, out of control, stretched ahead of her.

"What if I'm bad at being a mom?" She clenched the sheet in her hands. "What if this kid grows up to steal lunch money from her classmates and starts knocking over banks instead of going to college?"

"Nothing like high hopes, Rachel." He came back. His thighs brushed her leg and she tried to move away from him. He noticed with a pointed look, but said nothing. "I'll help you," he said. Saying yes would be so easy. "And Addie will be a great big sister. She'll whip this child into shape if you and I screw up."

"I can't afford to believe you want to stick around."

Frustration rippled across his face. "Even

if you never want to see me again, we are about to start raising a child together."

Another pain, impossible to ignore, ended the conversation. She reached for his hand, unwilling to need him, unable to deny herself the comfort of his touch.

"Any human would do right now," she said.

"I know." His nod might have hidden laughter or anger. She couldn't tell which.

SOON, RACHEL HURT TOO MUCH to snap at Andrew anymore. He missed it. He hadn't been around for Addie's birth, but Rachel's labor looked like a slow march to death.

The more she suffered, the quieter she grew. With her bottom teeth putting a dent into her upper lip, she was pale and wide-eyed and too damn strong for any woman's good.

"Scream again, Rachel. Swear and hate me."

She lifted tired eyes that only made him want to protect her more. "I'm doing all that in silence, believe me." Another pain erased her shaky smile. "I think something's different."

"What?"

"I don't know. It feels different. You'd better get the doctor."

"I don't want to leave you—"

"Go." She put some hatred into the word. He grabbed the compartment door, trying not to see his own shaking hand.

The older man had gone for a break and a tall glass of ice water Andrew envied as he found him with his wife and Addie. Andrew wiped his own dry mouth and laid his hand on Addie's small shoulder. "She says something's different."

The doctor didn't move, but Addie wrapped her arms around Andrew's waist. "I wanna see Rachel."

"In a little while, honey." Andrew hugged her and handed her back to the doctor's wife—all the while trying not to snatch Rachel's only port in this Christmas-train storm from his comfortable seat.

The doctor set his glass on the table between his seat and the one his wife was sharing with Addie. "I guess she might be ready to push."

Andrew felt the world tilt. What he knew about childbirth, they'd already surpassed, but pushing, he got. "Are you coming?" He must have asked it in a harsh tone. Three heads swerved his way. He tried to smile. "Now?" he asked.

"Let's go together." The doctor actually took his arm as if he needed assistance. "You know, women have been doing this for some time. Be careful or you'll scare your daughter."

"Our child is coming into the world on a train. Rachel's had no medication, and she looks like she's dying. Who knows how sanitary this place is?"

"Let's not borrow trouble."

"I won't let anything happen to her or the baby." What he meant was "Please don't let anything happen to the woman I love and the baby we've made together."

The doctor stopped. "They'll be fine. An ambulance is meeting us in Virginia City, and we'll be there in just a few hours."

"Not soon enough." He was the one who'd been too late. He could only pray Rachel would let him back into her life so that he could handle some more diapers and car seats and those damn inoculations.

"I WAS JUST LUCKY DR. TINSLEY was on the train, Maggie." After hours in pain, the lack of it left her exhausted, able only to stare with wonder and unbelievable, unending love at her own daughter, suckling at her breast.

"He rides this train every year." Maggie fluffed another pillow and eased it beneath the baby and Rachel's bent arm. "Your little sweet-pie isn't the first he's delivered."

"Kind of a Christmas tradition, then?"

Maggie smiled, but then tucked her hand around the baby's head. "I'd say she's one of a kind, wouldn't you?"

Rachel could only nod, too full of awe to answer. She felt small beside this much love. "Grace was worth it."

"Even having her father along?"

Honesty overtook Rachel. "I couldn't have done it without him. He was brave for me, and he let me be cranky when I had to be."

"That's all a man can do when his baby's coming." Maggie scooted the pillow to a more secure position. "Unless you're lucky enough to marry an OB. That'd be the smart thing."

Rachel laughed. The baby jumped and then settled again, finding comfort that astounded her mother. "Who knew I'd be comforting to anyone?" She didn't need an answer. Her ready bond with her daughter, a connection that deepened and warmed with each passing second, answered every question.

"Now that you're both clean and tidy, can I let Andrew and Addie in?" Maggie took the door handle. "The second I open this, they'll fall inside anyway so you might as well say yes."

"Yes." Rachel didn't know what came next—other than letting Andrew see his daughter. That part frightened her—sharing her baby with a long-distance father, but Addie... She couldn't wait to show off the baby to Addie—and vice versa.

Maggie opened the door to an empty hallway.

Rachel stared. Maggie lifted both eyebrows. "That's odd. I thought they'd be figuring ways to get the thing off its hinges."

"It's heartbreaking." She tried not to mind, but her hormones must be freaking. She wanted to cry. Trust Andrew to put distance between them now.

Maggie stepped into the hall, but then came back. She looked so uncertain, Rachel felt concerned.

"You asked Santa why he rides this train, but you never asked me," Maggie said.

"I thought it was your job."

"I have two children." Maggie turned the doorknob and it squeaked. "Two boys. They're with my mother right now, getting ready for Santa, trimming the tree, wrapping presents they've made for me."

Tears burned the back of Rachel's eyes.

"I have to take this trip. It's the best pay I get all year, and the bad decisions I've made—with their father—mean my boys need the extra money. I'll drive back to California all night and arrive with the morning, but my boys will have to wait to open their presents until I get there. They're always awake first."

"Is it that much money?"

The other woman nodded, staring at the floor. "It's my penance, and maybe I'm put on this train to remind women like you to keep your family safe. And together."

She was gone before Rachel could move to hug her or offer the slightest comfort.

"RACHEL WON'T CARE IF WE DON'T have flowers, baby."

"We're opposed to," his daughter said, *opposed* meaning *supposed* in Addie-speak.

"But there are no flowers in the dining car

and none in the bar." Where they'd looked at him as if he were a serial killer for bringing in his child.

"Let's ask Miss Maggie." In the narrow aisle between seats, Addie yanked on his arm, and, at the same time, rammed a guy's elbow into the sleeping young woman at his side.

"Sorry," Andrew said, as the man looked up, affronted. Then he saw the small bouquet at the woman's hip. "Can I buy those?"

"Dad," Addie said as if he'd struck the mother lode of good ideas.

"Do you know what time it is?" the man asked. The woman covered her flowers, protecting them.

Andrew glanced at his watch as he dug out his wallet with his other hand. "Six fifty-three. Can I buy your—" They must be newlyweds. Shiny rings, shinier faces. And she was acting as if those flowers had been hewn from gold. "Bouquet?"

"No," the girl said.

Andrew had already fished a fifty from his wallet. The new husband eyed it with reluctant avarice. "That's a lot of money for some used posies."

"Brad." The wife moved the flowers to

her other side, protecting them from her groom as well as Andrew.

"They're for my new sister's mommy," Addie said.

"Your sister's—" The bride stared at Andrew.

"My—" He wanted with all his heart to say *wife*. His stomach lurched, but he steeled himself and resorted to another tack. "My daughter believes we shouldn't show up empty-handed." He agreed, but he wanted to give Rachel a marriage license and a ring of her own. "I have another twenty-five in my wallet."

"No." The girl held out her flowers, reluctance in her extended wrist and her young eyes. Hadn't these kids possessed parents? They both looked too young for SATs, much less a wedding march. "You take these. Your wife must be the one who had the baby tonight."

Addie's accusatory stance made him want to confess all his sins. He held back and plucked a pink rose from the bouquet, which he handed back to the girl.

"Thank you," he said. "We had the baby." He turned Addie toward Rachel's compartment at last. "Let's hurry, little girl."

"You didn't tell her the truth. She thinks you and Rachel are married."

"Don't fight me now, Addie." She resisted moving so he scooped her into his arms. "Hold your feet in so you don't kick anyone in the head."

"Why don't you and Rachel get married?"

"You know I asked Rachel."

"You must have done something she didn't like. I want Rachel to be my mommy."

"I know." He meant to die trying, but he couldn't let Addie think they stood a chance. If Rachel hadn't given in, faced with a lifetime of single parenting, she might never find the will to trust him with her future.

He found Rachel's door, drumming on it harder than he'd intended. Some sound came from inside. Hardly a welcome.

"Let me down, Daddy."

With his pulse beating in his throat, he set Addie on the floor and restored her hard-won booty. The bunch of flowers looked bigger in her hand.

"Did she tell us to come in?" Addie asked.

"What else would she say?" That was his story, and he'd stick to it. Whatever she'd said hadn't sounded enthusiastic.

He opened the door. Addie rushed in, all but heaving the flowers at Rachel's head. "Lemme see, Rachel, lemme see!"

Rachel scooted backward so Addie could pile onto the bed beside her. Andrew tried to draw Addie back to keep her from hurting Rachel.

But the baby. She was even more gorgeous.

"She's Addie all over again." His own voice, cut by love and dread for all he might lose, hardly seemed to belong to him.

"Flowers?" Rachel held the baby for Addie to ooh over.

"Addie made me arm wrestle some guy for them." He wanted to grab them all in his arms and shut out the past and the future that loomed like an open wound of need without Rachel and his new baby in it.

"I thought you were staying away." Tears in her voice drew him at last from staring at the soft-faced infant she was cradling.

"I won't be able to, Rachel." He touched their baby's hand, only to have his index finger taken in a grip she'd need to fend off Addie's ready affection.

"Can I hold her?" His little girl was already reaching.

"Sit beside me, and you can help." Rachel, all soft and tired and young-looking in a clean pink nightshirt, eyed him over the children's heads. Then she had to pay attention to Addie. "Careful now. We can't hug too hard or we'll hurt her."

"I can't stay away from either of you. You're my family," Andrew said. "All of you."

CHAPTER EIGHT

IF ONLY HE'D SAID *WIFE* or *lover* or even *girl-friend*, for pity's sake. Family implied she was only the mother of his child—not an inconsequential position in any man's life, but not the only spot Rachel wanted to hold.

She wanted him to be blindly in love with her—as she'd been with him.

Alone with the girls while Andrew scouted for breakfast for her and Addie, Rachel looked from one sleeping child to the other. She couldn't love either of them more. Addie was as much hers as the new baby—as Grace. She'd always thought of the baby as Grace, despite it being Andrew's mother's name.

Maybe she'd wanted something of him in her life for always. He'd never abandon Grace.

The compartment door opened, and Andrew brought bagels and chocolate milk, the weakness she and Addie had often shared. Rachel had to smile so she averted her face.

"You'd better wake her." Addie was nestled in the arm she wasn't using to hold the baby. "I'm afraid I'll drop Grace."

Silence met her use of the baby's name. She'd avoided saying it since he'd first come back to the compartment. She'd give anything to take it back now.

"Grace?"

"I hear something in your voice." Still, she refused to look at him. "I like the name. That's all it means. Don't take it too seriously."

"You named the baby after my mother."

"If you don't like it—"

"Cut it out, Rachel. You know I'm glad."

"You sound angry."

"Because you're pretending we don't matter to each other. We don't have any more time to pretend. We have two girls who love us—who need a mother and father, and that's what you and I are to both of them."

She pressed her face to Addie's silky hair.

"It's not enough, Andrew. We aren't like those other families out there. I have to be an example to the girls, and an intelligent woman who values herself doesn't marry a man who only feels responsible toward her."

AN AMBULANCE MET THEM at the train depot and rocketed up the snow-laden hills to the hospital. By the time they'd had a few tests and been given a clean bill of health, Rachel's mother burst into the exam room from which Andrew and Addie had been evicted.

"Baby," Elizabeth Ford said, clearly mistaking Rachel for Grace. She wrapped her own daughter in her arms and then abruptly released her to scoop Grace out of her hospital-supplied bassinet. "She's perfect, Rachel. Absolutely, positively perfect. Good lord, how much she looks like Addie."

"Did you see her on your way in?"

"Sleeping with her daddy on those hard chairs out there." She looked up. "This sweet little morsel's daddy, too."

"Mom, don't start."

"You started this, you and that young man. You don't have sense to do the right thing. When I was a girl, we had a saying. You play, you pay."

"That was never a compassionate attitude, Mom."

"I agree, but maybe you should pay attention to its essential meaning."

"You're worried for me." Rachel slid off the examining table and began to dress. "You don't want me to be a single parent, and you're even a little afraid I might not be able to take care of my daughter on my own, because it was hard for you to care for me after Daddy died."

"Oh, a mind reader."

"But I've known from the start that I would be her only parent. I'm ready."

"You're full of—"

"Be careful. What if the baby retains a subliminal memory of the first words she hears you speak?"

Elizabeth laughed. "I'm a nice woman with delicate sensibilities, but I know you're fooling yourself. And so is Andrew. You loved each other. You didn't even leave him because you thought he didn't love you."

"That's exactly why I left. If he'd loved me, he'd have wanted children as much as I did."

With one hand, she helped Rachel back into her pink shirtsleeve. "He looks as exhausted as you. I guess neither of you slept?"

"We dozed after breakfast. Mom, he has to pick up presents for Addie. He left everything except her clothes in San Diego."

"We'll look after her while he shops."

"Thanks. I wanted to volunteer, but I couldn't without asking you because you'd have to help." Her mother's flash of triumph made her frown. "On my first day as a mother, hours after I've given birth."

"We'd better get out of here before the stores close." Elizabeth fished a thick blanket out of her suitcase-sized purse. "I brought this in case you needed it. What are we calling this dumpling?"

"Grace."

"Grace. Lovely. That's—"

"Andrew's mother's name, but it goes with Elizabeth...."

"You can name the next one after me. If Andrew's mother gets a baby, I should, too."

Rachel swathed Grace in the pale green blanket. "I didn't realize you knew so much about Andrew."

"I believed he was going to be my son-in-law. Grace and I have e-mailed a time or two."

No doubt to express mutual disapproval over their wayward children. Rachel had a bit more empathy for their feelings as she looked at Grace and imagined her own child in a similar pickle twenty-eight years from now.

She signed out and they started for the waiting room. Andrew rose, his smile broad for Elizabeth.

"This is your fault, too," she said, close to his ear.

"What's your fault, Daddy? Is Rachel's mommy mad at you?"

"I'm mad at Daddy and Rachel," Elizabeth said, kneeling beside Addie, "but not at you and your brand new sister. Will you come home with Rachel and Grace and me while your father goes out for a while?"

"I don't—know." She pushed a hand into her hair and glanced sideways at her father.

"We have to make cookies for Santa, and we need help trimming the tree," Rachel said. "And you can help me look after Grace."

"I need to pick up some things for your baby sister." Andrew helped Addie into her sweatshirt.

"I should help you. I know more what she needs 'cause we're almost the same age now."

Andrew smiled. "I think Rachel needs you more. She doesn't feel too well, and Santa likes a lot of cookies. She might need you to bring her Grace's diapers. And Elizabeth can't do the whole tree on her own. Who'll hand her the ornaments and help her string the lights?"

"I am good at all that." Addie reluctantly took Elizabeth's hand. "Oka-a-y. If you need me, I'd better stay with you and Rachel and Grace."

"We do need you." Elizabeth tucked Addie's hand against her side. "Do you think we should bake chocolate chip or peanut butter or oatmeal?"

"Choplate chip."

"How lucky am I? Santa likes my favorite kind." Elizabeth led Addie toward the doors.

"Let me take Grace," Andrew said to Rachel. "You look tired."

"According to my mother, you do, too." Nevertheless, she let him take the baby. She both hated and loved the sight of her daughter in Andrew's arms. Temptation whispered she could see them like this, like a family, any time.

It was a temporary dream, like Christmas itself.

THEY DISTRACTED ADDIE with the tree and cookies until Andrew came back with diapers and infant clothing and a red velvet coat Addie insisted on putting on the moment he pulled it out of the shopping bag.

"What about Gracie?" she demanded, fastening her wide black buttons.

"I got one for her, too." Andrew took out another red velvet garment, a snowsuit that looked small enough to fit Addie's doll.

"Is she that tiny?" Rachel asked.

"Yes, but she'll grow fast."

All but bounding from the discomfort of Rachel's guilty, wary silence, Elizabeth claimed she had the rest of the house to decorate. Soon after, Andrew went out to get more wood for the fireplace.

By the light of the Christmas tree and the flickering fire, Rachel nursed Grace and tried to imprint the sight of Addie, one elbow on her bent knee, one knee on the rug in front of the tree, peering into the stacks of presents.

"Are there any for me?" she asked.

"My mom says yes, and I have something for you." A silver tea set her mother had given her when she was Addie's age. She'd planned to give it to Addie anyway, and now she had the chance.

"Oh, don't tell me when it's under the tree. Last year, I went downstairs while you and Daddy were asleep and I peeled back the wrapping paper on some of the presents."

"Addie."

"Shhh." The little girl put one finger to her lips. "He'll be back any second. Don't tell him. I couldn't help it, but I'm growed up now."

Longing like hunger filled Rachel. She could see this moment replayed year after year, Christmas after Christmas. One day Addie would persuade Grace that Santa was coming, though she'd ceased to believe, herself.

Andrew came back, bringing cold and pine scent and another armload of firewood. Something in her eyes made him look at her twice.

"What?" he asked.

She couldn't find words without confessing her deepest want. He and Addie would make her whole.

Faint jingling bells wafted from the kitchen. Bolting upright as if she were on a spring, Addie swung to face them.

"Santa." Awe dropped her voice and glowed in her eyes.

Rachel envied her. If only a grown woman could believe so simply in what she wanted.

"Sleigh bells," Addie said. "I hear sleigh bells. It *must* be Santa."

"Addie, honey, come help me hang these?"

Rachel almost cried as her mother flourished the sleigh bells from the hall, bursting Addie's bubble. The little girl's face crumpled, but suddenly, she grinned.

"I'll bet Santa will hear those, and he'll know where to stop." She grabbed her father's sleeve. "Daddy, will Santa bring something for Grace? You think he knows about her?"

"Santa knows everything," Andrew said.

"I hope so, but I'd better make something for her, just in case. Grandma Elizabeth, do you have some crayons and some blank paper?"

Yet another silence played background to the crackling fire as Elizabeth's mouth straightened in a thin line. She swallowed several times before she spoke. "If I don't, we'll just go buy some for you and Grace."

She held out her hand to Addie, but then waited as the little girl skipped into the kitchen. "She called me Grandma," she said. "Grandma, Rachel."

"I heard."

"But did you listen? Do you know what it can mean?"

She left, and Rachel stole a look at Andrew, who had turned from stacking the wood to stare at Grace. His tender expression nearly undid Rachel.

She pushed to her feet more aware of every ache. "I need to change her diaper." She barely got the words out and then stumbled from the room, careful only to shelter Grace.

The telephone rang before she could make the stairs. She answered it in the hall.

"Rachel? This is Donna Roberts."

Donna Roberts and her family ran a program called the Santa Express that provided gifts and meals for families who might have gone without otherwise. She was always looking for volunteers. "Mrs. Roberts, how are you?"

"Not as fine as you if what I hear is more than gossip. Did you really have a baby on the Santa Superchief?"

"I did, but we're both well."

"I'm so glad. You know your mother has

been excited about the coming birth. Excellent Christmas present for her."

"For all of us," Rachel said, and that much was true. She might regret Andrew and their relationship, but she'd never regret the infant they'd made. "Do you want to speak to Mom?"

"If she's not busy."

"Mother." Rachel set down the phone, glad it had stopped her from running away. "Mrs. Roberts."

"Thanks, honey." The kitchen phone clattered as her mother apparently dropped it and then kicked it across the linoleum to Addie's delighted giggles. "You can hang up now. I've got it."

Rachel turned back to the living room. Andrew was still sitting on his haunches, staring at the flames.

"I'm not a coward," Rachel said.

"No." He brushed his hands down his thighs and she remembered similar moments, pushing him to the rug, chasing the stroke of his hands with hers, wanting him urgently because they'd been circumspect all day with Addie as an audience. "I have been," he said. "An idiot and a coward." He looked up. "But

I'm not now. I want you and my daughters. I want our family and I will not give up."

"Rachel?" her mother called, and Andrew stood. "Andrew," her mother went on, "that was my friend, Donna. She runs a—"

"Can I go, Daddy?" Addie asked, unable to wait for Elizabeth's explanation.

"Go where?" Andrew asked.

"I'm trying to tell you. My friend runs a charity called the Santa Express. Her family delivers Christmas gifts and meals tonight and then breakfasts in the morning for folks who can't get out. I've been helping since Rachel moved away. Apparently, she and her family have to be out of town tomorrow so she wanted to make sure I still planned to show up for my deliveries."

"And Grandma Elizabeth says I can go, too." Addie flung an arm around her father's waist. "Just like in *Little Women*."

Little Women? Rachel turned to Andrew. He stared between her and her mother, his face flushed.

"I thought all little girls were supposed to read that."

"Daddy read it to me," Addie said. "I liked Jo best, but Beth made me and Daddy cry."

Rachel couldn't look away from him. Her

mother, on the other hand, grabbed Addie and left the room.

"It made you cry, too?" Rachel asked.

"Beth had a hard life." He turned toward the kitchen. "If Addie's helping your mother in the morning, I'd better get her into bed. Don't make fun of me for trying to do the right thing."

"I can't picture you doing the voices, but I'd like to hear it. Do you need some help wrapping her gifts?"

"I had them do it at the stores." He headed for the kitchen.

Dumbfounded, she stared at sleeping Grace, peaceful and trusting in her arms. How could a man who'd been afraid of having more children cry over Beth March and talk about it?

"Andrew?"

He came back, but he didn't look as if he wanted to see her.

"I don't actually believe in stereotypes, but crying with your little girl is pretty brave."

"You never believed me, did you?"

"I thought it was one of the lamest excuses any guy ever invented."

"Nope. It was the truth. Then."

CHAPTER NINE

THE REST OF THE HOUSE was silent when Grace's newborn cries dragged Rachel out of sleep. Grimacing as she slid out of bed, she scooped the baby from the bassinet her mother had cleaned and set up in her room.

Gripping the banister with one hand, she eased down the stairs, anxious to keep the baby from waking anyone else. Her mother had never left the Christmas tree lights on when Rachel had been a child, but she'd left them on tonight for Addie.

Rachel settled into the armchair that had seen her through homework and phone marathons and daydreams of spending Christmases here with her parents and her own husband and children. Grace nursed hungrily while Rachel watched the tree's lights blinking.

"Can't sleep?"

"Mom, did we wake you?"

"I guess I'm as attuned to my baby as you are to yours."

Rachel grinned, but then licked her lips. "Will you get me a glass of water? I'm so thirsty."

Her mother went into the kitchen and returned with a glass of water she set at Rachel's elbow. "It's nursing. You need more fluids."

She nodded, sipping. "Will I do this one day? Bring water to my little girl as she's feeding her own infant?"

"If you're lucky."

Rachel hugged Grace closer. She already missed having the baby move inside her, but this was so much better, overwhelming, unconditional love that just was. Not like with Andrew, which was all tests and doubt. Shouldn't love between a man and a woman be this easy, too?

"Mom, I don't know how to believe in Andrew."

"You just do it."

"This is no Christmas movie where I see that he's a good dad to both his daughters, so I can jump in and hope he'll be a good husband, too. I want my girls—and in my heart, that means Addie, too—to believe they deserve a man who'll love them, not because it's right, but because he can't help himself."

"I'm not taking up for Andrew. I blame you both. You overcomplicated your lives, but what if he feels everything you need him to? He's come this far."

Rachel cradled the back of Grace's head. "I left him six months ago. He stopped calling. He never came. He can help himself."

"You ask too much. You say it's no Christmas movie, but you want the big romantic ending when what you really need is a beginning. Picture Andrew—"

"With someone else? I have."

"No, baby, alone. Imagine him alone. What if you are his one true love? A woman might excite him sexually one day. He might make friends at the playground with other mothers, but say he loves only you. Imagine him alone every Christmas Eve of his life. You love him. You want him to be happy. Do you want to be the reason for his loneliness?"

"The movies you watch are sad."

"You may be making one of those for Andrew and for your girls. Think about that."

ANDREW HESITATED AT THE TOP of the stairs. He could go down now and argue with both women and wake Gracie or he could let Rachel rest and offer her his love in the first light of Christmas morning.

Her mother was wrong. He wanted to tell her—make them both see they had a cockeyed view of the future.

But tomorrow would be better, when Addie and Elizabeth were delivering Christmas meals and he'd have Rachel and Gracie to himself. Her mother had applied as much pressure as he had. Rachel could use a break.

He went back to his room. In a little while Rachel and Elizabeth came upstairs. With whispered goodnights, they returned to their beds, too. He resisted a compulsion to see his new daughter safely into her bassinet. He'd never had to share Addie. That would take getting used to.

Night crept by, second by second. From the open door of the room next to his, Addie's soft snoring kept Andrew company until dark blue light crept into the snow-heavy sky.

He was just drifting off when his door swung open and Addie leaped onto his bed.

"It's time." Her whisper probably raised the roof. "Santa came—we gotta wake up Gracie and Rachel!"

He persuaded her to let Rachel and the baby sleep, as they'd been up during the night. And on second thought, Addie decided it would be more like *Little Women* if she didn't open any of her presents until she and her "Grandma Elizabeth" delivered their breakfasts.

Elizabeth came to the door. Andrew signaled to her that he'd help Addie dress. Soon, the woman and the little girl left hand in hand.

As soon as Grace began to whimper, he hurried to the kitchen and poured a glass of orange juice, which he ran upstairs to Rachel's room.

"I'm up, Mom. Did Grace cry?"

"Not yet," Andrew said. He put the juice on her nightstand as she sat up, covering herself with her blankets.

Andrew went to the bassinet, loving Grace's absorbed stare.

"Morning, sweet one," he said. "Ready to eat?" He glanced at Rachel. "Not making a bottle seems strange."

"I'm already getting a little sore. The

nurse at the hospital said I would, though."
She stopped as if she wished she hadn't said
that. "What are you doing in here?"

"We have to talk. You know we do."

"I thought you'd eventually say so." Her
anxious eyes followed Grace's waving
hand. "She must be hungry again."

He passed her their baby. "I heard you
and your mother last night."

"What?"

"She was right about one thing."

Rachel must have forgotten she was feeling
modest around him, because she lifted Grace
to her breast with no shyness. "I know you'll
learn to care about someone else."

"No." He handed her the juice. "You need
more fluids."

Rachel laughed, her eyes wide. "I keep
forgetting you're like this."

"Like what?" Pathetically, he wanted her
to say something nice about him.

"Easy to be with. Funny."

"You always said laughing was foreplay."

She turned to Grace, blushing, and he
enjoyed the slightest revenge for her amuse-
ment at his reading material.

"We might not have had you, little girl, if
I didn't get your father's jokes." She

stopped, but only for a second, and her gaze accused him. "You eavesdropped."

"And I wanted to argue."

"But you held back. You always hold back."

"Usually when I think I'm wrong, but this time, I knew I was right, and I wanted to talk to you alone." He brushed her hair behind her ear. She shivered, and he forgot to breathe. His touch still affected her. "I don't want you to come to me because you're afraid I'll learn to love someone else or I'll be alone."

She looked up, but he knelt beside her. Grace complained and he realized he was leaning on Rachel's thigh.

"I loved you without learning how," he said. "I just love you. Because you took me on with Addie, because you called me first when you had good news, because you fought so hard to stay with me when I got scared." He rubbed his head. "I'm saying this badly. Remember all those bedtime stories? We'd both be yawning wide enough to break our jaws by the time Addie fell asleep, but then we fell into bed with each other, and we made love with urgency. We never stopped needing each other. That's not something you learn."

"But it doesn't promise a future either."

He shook his head. "I don't want you to choose me because you're afraid of losing me. I want you to come home because you love me. I need you to be my wife and want our girls—because Addie's as much yours as Grace is mine."

"I know we both want our family."

He rose and caught the nape of her neck. She opened her mouth to protest. He kissed her with need he'd suppressed for nearly a year. Only when the baby caught him a swift kick in the sternum did he lean back, rubbing his chest.

His voice was so thick he could barely speak. "She's protective."

"What are you doing?"

"Telling you the truth. I love you. I want you. I need you. And by the way, I love our daughters, too."

"How do I believe you, Andrew?"

Hope surged, almost as strong as Gracie's left foot. "You just do, the way Addie believes in Santa, despite Joey's best efforts to persuade her he's fake."

"That's it, Andrew. You persuaded me you were fake, but I started thinking you might not be when I was in labor."

He kissed her again. "I'm not fake, now. I'm cured." He rubbed his chest again, drinking Grace in as if he had to make memories of her. "You just wait until that first doctor's appointment. You're going to be scared, too. They poke at them and…"

"Don't tell me." She pulled him close, kissing his chin, brushing his cheek with her eyelashes. "Maybe it *would* be easier with you along."

"You take any excuse that eases your pride over the hump. I know you love me."

"You do?" Her eyes asked him how.

"I trust you."

"Daddy?" Addie called from downstairs.

"Did you hear that front door open?" he asked, wishing they'd had a few more minutes to themselves.

Addie took the stairs as fast as she could, but she skidded to a halt in Rachel's open door. "You're coming home with us," she said.

Rachel laughed, and she put her arm around Andrew's shoulder. Feeling pride in her possession, he brought her hand to his lips. Again, she shivered.

"I believe in choosing what we both want, rather than choosing you because I'm afraid of being alone. I can do it for you all."

Rachel looked at him, her eyes honest and open and hopeful. "I believe I can."

"I believe, too, in you and me." He held out his other hand for Addie. "Come see Grace."

She climbed onto his bent knees, her little feet hardly pressing into his thighs. "Doesn't that hurt, Rachel?"

"No. You'll do it one day when you have a baby."

"Yuck." Addie curled her lip and jumped down. "I have to go tell Grandma."

"Tell her what?" Rachel asked.

"That we're going to be together all the Christmases from now on."

She bounded from the room.

Andrew resisted a moment's fear and searched the face of the woman he'd loved and almost lost. "Are you sure you're okay with that?"

Rachel quirked her index finger beneath his chin. "Kiss me again and we'll start the future." She pressed her forehead against his. "But hurry. Those two downstairs are soul mates. One of them will drag the other back any second."

* * * * *

New York Times *bestselling author
Linda Lael Miller is back
with a new romance featuring
the heartwarming McKettrick family
from Silhouette Special Edition.*

SIERRA'S HOMECOMING
by Linda Lael Miller

*On sale December 2006,
wherever books are sold.*

Turn the page for a sneak preview!

Soft, smoky music poured into the room.

The next thing she knew, Sierra was in Travis's arms, close against that chest she'd admired earlier, and they were slow dancing.

Why didn't she pull away?

"Relax," he said. His breath was warm in her hair.

She giggled, more nervous than amused. What was the matter with her? She was attracted to Travis, had been from the first, and he was clearly attracted to her. They were both adults. Why not enjoy a little slow dancing in a ranch-house kitchen?

Because slow dancing led to other things. She took a step back and felt the counter flush against her lower back. Travis naturally came with her, since they were holding hands and he had one arm around her waist.

Simple physics.

Then he kissed her.

Physics again—this time, not so simple.

"Yikes," she said, when their mouths parted.

He grinned. "Nobody's ever said that after I kissed them."

She felt the heat and substance of his body pressed against hers. "It's going to happen, isn't it?" she heard herself whisper.

"Yep," Travis answered.

"But not tonight," Sierra said on a sigh.

"Probably not," Travis agreed.

"When, then?"

He chuckled, gave her a slow, nibbling kiss. "Tomorrow morning," he said. "After you drop Liam off at school."

"Isn't that…a little…soon?"

"Not soon enough," Travis answered, his voice husky. "Not nearly soon enough."

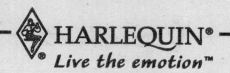
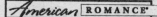

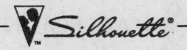